OWN

Sienna Snow

CHAPTER ONE

Damon

GLASS AND STEEL, cold and lifeless, unique, a feat of modern design, with no other structure possessing the same elements.

That's how magazines and critics described my buildings around the world.

They were full of shit and knew nothing.

They were ice palaces—glass and steel, cold and lifeless, with no warmth or feeling, just like my existence.

With my back against the balcony railing, I sat on the floor and stared at the two-story structure, representing the pinnacle of all I'd accomplished.

I threw my glass across the terrace. "This place is junk compared to her."

She was all that I ever wanted, needed, desired.

The only woman I ever loved.

My Sophia.

And I destroyed her. I broke her. I betrayed her trust.

She was better off without me.

I closed my eyes and lifted my face to the sky. The bright morning sunlight beamed down on me, making me squint and my head spin.

I wasn't sure how many days I'd spent out here, maybe two. It was probably a lot more since I remembered getting up a few times to accept takeout orders.

At least I managed to eat something.

I glanced through the floor-to-ceiling panels making up the wall separating the living room of my penthouse and my terrace. Food boxes sat on every surface, as well as dirty dishes.

The moment I tore apart the one good thing in my life, I abandoned the desire for control and order. Chaos was what I deserved.

It wouldn't matter to anyone what happened to me anyway. I might as well continue my tumble into obscurity.

I'd lost all the people who cared about me.

Who gave a shit if I'd picked up a bottle for the first time in my life to see if the oblivion my father and grandfather loved so much actually existed?

Yeah, it existed, but it made you remember

every other damn thing you fucked up in your life even more.

At least now I understood why the bastards kept hitting the bottle. It made them forget what pieces of shit they were for that short time the haze had its hold on them. Not to mention nausea and the hangover.

Why the hell would anyone want to feel this way?

"You're a liar, Damon Pierce. And know this. I will hate you forever for doing this to us."

The memory of Sophia's tear-streaked face as she'd said those words filled my mind.

That was why? It was better to suffer the hangover, the horrendous pain of remembering the loss of the most important thing in your life.

I reached for my tumbler of fifty-year-old scotch and realized there wasn't anything near me.

"Goddammit." I pushed to my knees. "Whose bright idea was it to throw the glass at the door?"

Fuck. I was talking to myself.

And what the hell was that smell?

It was me.

Jesus, I needed a shower.

I had to get my head back on straight.

Slowly, I managed to stand and staggered into the penthouse. Bracing my hand on a nearby wall,

I took in the mess I'd created over the week since the infamous night at the club where I obliterated my future.

Empty bottles sat on various spots everywhere, along with food containers. An odor of something unpleasant lingered in the air, hinting of decay, and my dirty discarded clothes amassed in small piles on any available surface.

I ran a hand through my hair.

I'd gone from needing everything immaculately clean to living in a damn pigsty. My cleaning crew would quit the minute they stepped into the front entryway.

Then again, maybe I'd leave it this way. It wasn't as if anyone would come to check on me.

Unless it was to put a bullet in my head, there wasn't a fat chance in hell that Lucian Morelli would grace me with his presence.

I'd broken the cardinal rule when it came to the man I considered my brother in all things but blood. I went behind his back and not only dated his baby sister but broke her heart.

It wouldn't matter if my reasons for doing it were honorable. I'd hurt her, and to Lucian, that was all that mattered.

He'd warned me, so I deserved the hit he, more than likely, had contracted out on me.

Not only had I lost him as a friend, but everyone else in our small circle. We were all tied to Lucian's club, Violent Delights. I was no longer a member there.

Membership revoked for breaking the rules. One rule in particular was to respect a submissive's safeword.

It was better this way.

Stepping further into the living room, I shook my head to clear the nauseating scent of rotting food.

I canceled the earlier thought of leaving this place in its current state. This filth had to go. What the hell was I thinking?

I wasn't.

At least I could say I'd lived through my first-ever alcoholic bender and never planned to do it again.

I'd find another vice.

It wouldn't be kink. I'd lost all access to the club and the social connections I'd garnered there. It wouldn't matter on that end, anyway. The thought of that place left an unsettled feeling in my gut.

By avoiding clubs, I wasn't a danger to anyone. There were no risks of me going too far, no worries of losing myself to my demons, no rumors to make anyone question my motives.

Besides, I couldn't imagine stepping inside Violent Delights unless Sophia walked by my side. No other woman could compare to her, her beauty, presence, and smart mouth that never gave an inch. I couldn't fathom the idea of touching anyone but her. She'd ruined me for any other woman.

Sooner or later, she'd find someone better, someone more suited for her, someone who wouldn't push her past her limits or hurt her, someone who could give her all she needed and deserved.

I gritted my teeth, hating the mere thought of anyone grazing their fingers even slightly across an inch of her skin.

I was the first man ever to touch her, take her innocence, give her pleasure, and show her the beauty of her sexuality. I corrupted and ruined her for me, not any fucking body else.

She was fucking mine.

I growled and resisted the urge to smash my hand through the wall near me. Instead, I took hold of a pizza box and headed into my kitchen, tossing the greasy container in the garbage can.

Fuck me. The kitchen wasn't any better than the rest of the house.

Where the hell to start?

Just looking at the place added to the throbbing in my head. Maybe I was still drunk. Who the fuck knew?

Before even attempting to tackle the mess around me, I had to find something to relieve the pounding in my head.

Ten minutes later, after a fruitful search for ibuprofen and downing three glasses of water, I held a few trash bags and focused on the project ahead of me.

"Time to purge this monstrosity."

I'D BARELY WASHED the shampoo out of my hair when my ability to ignore the consistent buzzing of the intercom shattered. The fact I let my phone die was a big enough hint to leave me the fuck alone. But it looked as if the dickhead downstairs wasn't getting the memo.

Which meant it was the one and only Lucian Morelli.

I might as well allow him to put me out of my misery. I felt no better now than when I'd woken up after passing out on the terrace.

Washing the suds from my face, I ended my shower and reached for my towel.

The intercom continued to blare while I shrugged on a pair of lounge pants, and then I couldn't help but groan when the emergency phone in the kitchen rang, died down, and started up again.

For the love of God, I wasn't dead. I decided to drop out of sight for a little while.

I scanned my place, still seeing a less-than-stellar reflection of its former self.

At least it no longer reeked of decaying food and alcohol.

Moving to the front entryway, I punched in the code to allow access to my private elevator and waited.

Less than three minutes later, the cab opened to reveal my expected guest of honor.

He looked me up and down. A disgusted sneer appeared on his face, and then he shook his head.

"Go ahead. Do your worst." I opened my arms wide.

Instead of punching me in the face as I expected, he shoved past me and strode into my place.

"What? Don't you want to shoot me or maim me in some way? Here's your chance. I'll make it easy on you and won't move."

"It takes the joy out of it if you don't fight back. Nobody wants an easy mark." Lucian glanced over his shoulder. "You look like shit. Put on a shirt, for fuck's sake."

"Since the last thing on my agenda for the day was entertaining, I give two shits about making a good first impression."

"I'm not here for a social visit."

"Then what the hell do you want? Either beat me up or leave. I don't have time for you."

"You're making time." Lucian continued into the penthouse and abruptly stopped as his focus landed on a near-empty bottle of his favorite fifty-year-old scotch sitting on a corner of the bar in the living room. "Interesting. You are mortal, after all."

"Want to elaborate?"

"I expected to find you at work, lost in designing the latest and greatest structure the world has ever seen. Not like this."

I clenched my jaw. "What do you mean by this?"

"Don't even pretend you don't know what I mean. Your preferred method of coping with your troubles is to work yourself to the limit. Then when you resurface, you've created some cold, architectural fortress only other assholes can appreciate." Lucian moved to the bottle of nine-thousand-dollar scotch, picked it up, grabbed a tumbler, and poured a serving for himself. "But here you are, recovering from what looks like a bender."

"What's your point?"

Ignoring my question, he lifted his glass in my direction as if giving me a toast. "At least you can say you spent your last week wasted on scotch that was older than our parents and worth more than most people's mortgages for three months."

"Get out. I lived it. No need for the recap."

Lucian downed his drink and walked past me into my kitchen as if he owned my fucking penthouse. He opened my refrigerator, grabbed a water bottle, and tossed it to me.

"Drink it. Assholes who never indulge don't know how to handle the aftermath. I'll have a recovery formula here in twenty minutes." Lucian pulled out his phone, texted, and smirked in my direction.

"You're loving this."

"Why the fuck shouldn't I? You deserve every second of the misery."

"Let me repeat if you aren't here to kill me, get the fuck out. I don't want company. What I want is solitude. As in, goodbye. I want to be alone."

"Too fucking bad, Pierce. We're going to have a chat. Sit your ass down."

"I'm not one of your underlings, Morelli. You can't order me to do anything. Leave your magic formula with the reception desk downstairs and get lost."

"That's right, rules don't apply to you." Lucian clenched his hands. "You hurt Sophia."

"I did." I ran a frustrated hand through my hair. "I'll admit it. I'm the epitome of what you surmised. I'm dangerous and the wrong person for her. I'm everything the rumors about me say. I own it. I'm the worst thing that could have ever happened to her."

"Oh, cut the dramatic martyr crap."

"It's the truth. I pushed Sophia. I hurt her."

"You did it on purpose. I heard the audio."

"You're a sick fuck if you listened to your sister having sex."

"That wasn't sex, jackass. You staged the ending. Not once did you want it to go the way it did. You escalated it for a purpose, even if you hated every single aspect of it."

"I don't need your analysis."

The pounding intensified, making me wish I never unlocked the elevator.

"You have it. What was the point of the whole thing?"

I might as well let him hear the truth. I was too exhausted to deny it anyway.

I slid onto a barstool and admitted, "To prove everything said about me was true. I'm not right for her. I'm not good for her. She deserves better. I'm too intense. You said it yourself. I push my subs to places where they forget to protect themselves. I enjoy going to that edge, and I make it addictive."

"That's bullshit." Lucian set his palms on the island across from me and leaned in with irritation etched on his face. "Do you believe I'm any different? All of my relationships have bordered on that edge you talk about. I don't know any other way. Hell, I don't want any other way. I can honestly say my demands, the way I am, made Elaine stronger."

"Maybe it's safer with you. Your way isn't getting your women hurt. I'm dangerous to mine. Look at my damn track record. It speaks for itself. It's better not to play anymore."

He shot me a skeptical glare. "Ever? I don't buy it."

Without Sophia, I never wanted to enter any club again, but I kept those thoughts to myself.

"Ever."

"Are you telling me that you never plan to f—"

Lucian stopped speaking when the elevator dinged, indicating someone arrived.

Who the fuck could that be?

A second after the cab doors opened, Eva Morelli stepped out. The heavily pregnant woman carried an extra-large designer tote filled to capacity in one hand and her purse in the other.

I narrowed my eyes at Lucian. "Is this a damn Morelli invasion?"

Ignoring me, Lucian stalked toward Eva, grabbed her bags, and demanded. "What the hell are you doing here? Isn't there a wedding in less than a week requiring your attention?"

"Hey, jackass, since this is my place, should I be the one asking questions to my visitors?"

"Shut up, Pierce. She is my sister. Therefore, I'm in charge." Lucian's attention returned to Eva. "Answer the damn question."

"You're in charge. Really?" Eva rolled her eyes. "And to answer your nicely worded question. Isn't it obvious? I'm here to kick the ass of the man who broke our baby sister's heart."

Immediately, I remembered the pain and devastation on Sophia's face as she walked away from me. She believed I'd broken her heart at the moment, but soon, she would realize she'd escaped with her life.

I'd lured her into my web as I'd done to my other subs. She deserved so much better than anything I could offer her.

"What do you have in here?" Lucian lifted the overflowing bag. "It weighs a ton."

"Resources. Bring it to the kitchen and set it on the counter."

"Whatever you plan to bring about my ultimate demise has to be better than his plan to psychoanalyze me. I'd rather endure torture."

We both followed her in.

Once Lucian set the tote down, Eva unzipped it.

I opened my arms as I'd done when Lucian arrived. "Do your worst."

"So dramatic. No wonder the two of you are friends." Eva removed a set of covered dishes from the bag and placed them on the island.

"We're not friends," Lucian countered. "What the hell is all of that? Are you planning to poison him?"

"I originally planned to redecorate this ice palace, as Sophia calls it, by flinging the food I brought all over the place, but looking at him, I think I'll feed him."

Lucian hummed, "That's not a bad idea considering how poison was a nice plot point in the murder scenario Sophia lived through over the last few months."

"This is the worst fucking invasion, intervention, whatever, in the history of the planet." The pounding in my head intensified, making me wish to heaven one of them had shot me. "I thought you Morellis were hardasses, not bleeding hearts offering water bottles and bringing casseroles. What the ever-loving fuck?"

"I have no heart. In fact, I feel nothing. Or did you forget?" Lucian's deadpan response had Eva shoving his shoulder.

"Whatever. You are the most volatile of all of us. You only pretend to feel nothing."

Interesting.

It looked as if Eva wasn't in on the little secret about her brother. Emotionally, Lucian ran the gamut of feelings. However, when it came to the physical side of life, I could stab the asshole, and he wouldn't know it.

"While the two of you continue your discussion, I'll go clean up my terrace. It's a mess." I turned, ready to leave the siblings to their madness, and then grabbed hold of the island as a wave of nausea hit my stomach.

How the fuck had the jackasses in my family suffered like this and continued to drink all day, every day?

"I think you need to get some food into your system. It will help absorb any remaining alcohol in your stomach and lessen the hangover you are obviously suffering." Eva stepped in front of me. "Let's go in the living room and have a chat while Lucian heats the food."

"When the hell did I become the kitchen staff? And what makes you think I know anything about reheating gnocchi?" Lucian's surly reaction made listening to Eva's instructions worth it.

"If you did it for Elaine during her pregnancies, you can do it now."

Instead of waiting for his response, she took my arm and directed me into my living room.

These Morellis took over without giving two shits what anyone thought about a situation.

Sophia had infiltrated every part of my mind from the second our eyes connected from across the club, and I'd never been the same.

Once Eva and I sat on one of my long sofas, a series of curses reached us.

Eva smirked, and I shook my head. "Only you and Elaine can order him about, and he doesn't threaten to kill you."

"Don't forget Sophia. She'd pull a gun on him before he realized what happened. Besides, Lucian knows better if he wants me to feed him."

Her observation about Sophia reminded me of the many times she took none of my crap and gave me whenever I annoyed her.

"Sophia said you never drink. Was this a lie?" Eva asked, studying me.

Well, it was more of an inspection of everything about me, and she seemed completely unfazed by the fact I wore only my lounge pants.

"For thirty-five years, I hadn't."

"And what made you change your mind?"

My heart clenched. "I decided to stop fighting my nature and accept it."

"Hmm." A crease formed between her brows. "So it doesn't have to do with you trying to numb the pain of walking away from Sophia?"

I dropped my head into my hands. "Jesus, another Morelli here to play shrink."

"She knows what you did in the club was intentional."

"Was that a question?"

"Okay, have it your way. Here is a statement and a question. You love each other. Am I wrong?"

I looked at her. "She doesn't even know me. I keep her in the high of subspace, and she mistakes it for love. She couldn't even protect herself from me."

Eva snorted. "You think highly of your cock, don't you?"

"Of course, he does. He is Dom Damon. Every sub wants a piece of him." Lucian strode into the living room, wiping his hands on a cloth. "Too bad he's given all of it up now. Want to tell Eva why?"

"No, I'd rather you get lost."

"I'm warming up Eva's famous gnocchi for you. The hell if I'm leaving without enjoying a plate of it." He took a spot in an armchair across from me.

"Circling back to Sophia," Eva interjected. "You're not giving her enough credit. She survived in our family. We grew up in the epitome of toxic childhoods. She protected herself from the abuse of our parents."

"The two of you and Leo stepped in. She told me."

Surprise flashed across Eva's face, and she shot a quick glance at Lucian before refocusing on me. "She shared things about our family with you?"

I nodded, feeling the burning deep in my gut.

"Then she must have told you how she protected herself in the dangerously competitive fashion and modeling world?" Eva posed her words as a question, but I knew it was a statement.

"I know everything that happened to her. She's the strongest woman I've ever encountered."

"So let me get this straight. Sophia is strong enough to survive our insane family, her ruthless career, her invasive public life, but not a relationship with you, even if it entails kink?" Eva stood, moving around me and toward my kitchen. "You do think highly of your magic cock. For a smart man, you're very stupid. Come on, it's time to eat."

"You heard the pregnant lady, let's eat. Then you need to go fix things with our baby sister."

CHAPTER TWO

Sophia

"SOPHIA, SOPHIA, SOPHIA. I'm not sure whether to worry or applaud you on this collection you are designing."

I pulled a safety pin from between my lips and cocked a brow at my dear friend, Karina Mehta. She studied the five detailed sketches pinned to the large board on the wall. Her fashion designer eye missed nothing, and from the way she scrutinized every aspect of my unique outfits, she had opinions to share with me.

She arrived in my newly rented studio space about ten minutes ago. Before even giving me a courtesy hello, she pushed past me, trekking directly to inspect the products of her teachings from the years of our friendship.

Since I loved and appreciated her feedback, I asked, "Care to elaborate on that comment?"

She remained quiet for a few more minutes. This was her normal process. She thought things through and then spoke.

And I returned to pinning a section of fabric to the shoulder strap of one of the garments I worked on. I planned to build this piece in sections, eventually turning it into a formfitting black and red bodysuit consisting of a corset meant to exaggerate the waistline and accentuate the derrière.

The model who wore this ensemble would need attitude and confidence—the goddess embodying fierce domination.

There was another thing to add to my never-ending to-do list: make time to select the people to walk for the fashion show. Maybe I could ask my sisters and sisters-in-law to join the show. They were gorgeous and the perfect variation in body types for the collection.

Who was I kidding? The moment their significant others, meaning my brothers, found out, they'd nix the idea. I could always ask... at least I had Lizzy on the line. She'd never say no to me.

A tingle of butterflies settled in my stomach, along with a bit of anxiety. Karina was the first to see any part of this collection, my vision, and how I wanted the world to see me now.

As if reading my thoughts, she asked, "I'm wondering what you want to get out of this collection. Do you have a goal?"

"Tell me what you are reading from my designs."

"It isn't about what I'm reading but how you answer this question. Is this your way of saying I accept myself in all of myself, including the rebel and the wild child, or are you skirting the edge of acceptable to make a stir and fuck with people?"

I lifted my gaze to the designs, feeling the energy they churned inside me.

This had nothing to do with anyone but me, the girl growing into the woman, the bud blooming into a flower, the innocent learning her true sexuality.

"I'm Sophia Morelli. Isn't it my job to fuck with people?"

"Seriously, what's the motivation behind this? You're so driven. The bags under your eyes tell me you are in that manic, completely focused mode when inspiration takes over. I've been there, so I know the signs."

If she only knew how right she was. Over the last week and a half, I'd lost myself in creating something for the next Fashion Week. I refused to wait for another season. There was no more dreaming, no more someday. My day was here and now.

Wasn't it amazing how heartbreak and loss sparked a fire under a girl's ass? Every ounce of pain, every experience, every pent-up feeling of rage, sadness, and lingering love flowed into my creations.

I held Karina's knowing eyes, letting her see the cascade of emotions churning inside me. "For the first time in my life, I'm doing something that focuses solely on what I love. This is my art. I had a vision, and this is the product. I needed to set it free, which is what I'm doing. I don't care if I upset my family or anyone. Deep down inside, these pieces are what I see showcased on the runway."

Karina nodded, a wisp of a smile touching her full lips. "It looks like I have some competition in the pushing boundaries department."

I gave an unladylike snort, moved away from the piece on the table, and came to stand beside Karina. "I highly doubt this. You win with your million-dollar gem-filled lingerie. These are conservative in comparison."

"Sorry to disappoint you, but"—she pointed to various images—"your titles alone will catch headlines. *The Virgin, Princess, Pet, Little Girl, and Brat*. I can't wait to see what you name the rest of the items in the collection."

My attention settled on the form surrounded and draped with all the fabric and supplies for the set I called the *Little Girl*. Once finished, the dress and accessories would give a vibe mixing the look of a schoolgirl playing dress up during playtime. The whole thing was inspired by Daddy/little scenes I watched during my time as a voyeur at Violent Delights.

I focused back on Karina and smirked. "I learned from the queen of marketing, Madame Mehta. We have to fill the seats to wow them with the product."

"Oh, my little caterpillar is morphing into a butterfly," Karina gushed, setting a hand over her heart. "Man, why didn't I think of using the concept of BDSM as an aesthetic in my designs? The way you've incorporated the subtle styling of ropes and collars mixed in with chains is perfect. And this whip and handcuff belt, if you had a demo made, I'd steal it right now to wear."

I grinned. My heart swelled hearing this kind of praise from Karina. She wasn't the easiest person to impress. She had an eye for detail and held no punches if she saw room for improvement.

"So you like it?"

"You did good, my little butterfly." She patted

my head, and we both laughed, then all of a sudden, her face grew serious. "Don't tell anyone what you are planning. Keep a lid on this whole thing until you're ready to present. You know my history. Learn from my mistakes."

I released a breath. "I have. People like Keith Randolph won't get a chance in hell to steal my designs. You and my siblings are the only people aware of my plans."

I refused to allow anyone to stand in the way of my future. Over the last few months, I'd overcome so many things. Among the top on the list was being falsely accused of the jackass predator Keith's murder. Oh, and then there was the nearly being killed by a woman Keith's father hired to eliminate me. Yeah, maybe that should go before my arrest.

Jesus, I seriously needed a break from life.

I snapped out of my thoughts when Karina said, "May that bastard rest in hell. I hope that poison made his last moments in life as painful as possible."

"If I had a drink. I'd toast to that."

"That man caused so many women so much pain." The way Karina clenched her jaw told me the scars he'd left on her had yet to heal.

After my acquittal of Keith's murder and the

very publicized investigation into Randolph Senior's bribery and coverup scandal, dozens of Keith's victims came out to tell their stories. That horrible man had used his father's affluence and money to cover up decades of assaults and rapes. Both father and son had ruined so many lives with blackmail and career defamation.

Even Henrietta Stanford, the bitch who framed me for killing Keith, was his victim. He was her business partner in a textile design endeavor and then stole her work out from under her and passed it off as his. He took the credit and profit for all of Henrietta's work, leaving her out in the cold.

"Is it wrong that I feel compassion for that horrible woman who pinned Keith's murder on me?" I stared straight ahead of me, not really seeing anything, just letting my eyesight blur for a moment. "It isn't as if I forgive her, but in a twisted sort of way, I get why she did it."

"No. Keith victimized her, and his father covered up his predatory behavior. What she did to you was fucked up in so many ways, but in the end, her desperation caused her to use Keith's obsession with you as her escape plan."

"Some people still think I offed him." I shook my head at the continued rumors swirling around the fashion industry about me.

"She confessed in great detail how she did it. What more do the idiots want?"

I glared at her. "They think my family paid her off to take the fall for me."

"If people are stupid enough to believe a successful entrepreneur would take the wrap for you, which includes a plea deal and a ten-year stint in prison while her business flounders, then more power to them."

"I suppose you're right. I'm just exhausted from everything. After what I've gone through over the last few months, my circle of trust is very limited."

"And your man, where is he in this equation?" Karina strode to a form holding the completed ensemble design I'd named the Pet and fingered the leather collar. "Don't you trust him? After all, he is the one who gave you the deep dive into the world of kink."

Acid burned the back of my throat as I watched Karina finger the leash-like boa attached to the collar of the gown and then trail her fingers down the faux fur mix collar of the robe, hanging on a rack near it.

After a few heartbeats, I said, "We aren't together anymore."

Even now, after so many days of shedding tears and working through the roller coaster of everything that had happened between Damon and me, it felt as if it was only yesterday that he'd thrown what we'd had away.

"No, I don't believe it. It makes no sense. I saw the two of you together. Your chemistry was off the charts and intense."

"Believe it." I swallowed down the pain filling my chest. "He chose this, not me."

Karina wrapped an arm around my shoulder and squeezed me to her. "Men are idiots. He's going to regret it."

"Yeah, well, I'm not waiting around for that day. I have too many things to accomplish. I refuse to let anything hold me back any longer."

"That's my girl. Channel it all into your career."

"Spoken like a true workaholic."

She shrugged her shoulders. "I won't deny it."

"Hey, I have an idea." I touched my lip with my index finger.

Karina narrowed her eyes. "I'm not sure I'm going to like this."

"Of course, you are, since it will make you money."

"Okay, I'm listening."

"How about letting me use some of your jewelry as accent pieces in my collection? This way, it ratchets up the show's ambiance a notch."

"Oh, like a preview for my collection to draw people to my show."

"Exactly."

"My little jailbird comes up with the best ideas."

I glared at her. "What happened to the butterfly? I was acquitted, remember? Not jailbird, butterfly."

"Diva is more like it. Come on, show me some more concepts you're working on for the next batch of designs."

"Whatever you say, oh great teacher."

"Don't even think about it, Sophia Donatella Morelli."

I glared at Mom as I made the last-minute adjustment to the cleavage of Eva's gown and then smiled up at my beautiful sister.

"For your information, I'm trying to keep her girls covered. I think she grew a cup size in the last two days. Jesus, Eva. Please do me a favor and don't go into labor before you say your vows. That lady over there will say I'm the reason my nephew was born out of wedlock."

Eva gave me a beaming smile and winked at me, leaning down. "I'll let you in on a little secret if you promise not to say anything to, you know who."

We both sneaked a peak at Mom, who busily fussed at the stylist working on Lizzy's hair for the wedding.

"I have a feeling I know what you are about to say, so let me hear it."

"Finn and I took care of the deed a few months ago. All of this." She gestured around her. "Is all a formality."

I lifted a brow. "I hope you know I plan to collect for making me suffer through multiple fittings with mommy dearest."

"I have no doubt." Eva wrapped her arms around my shoulders and drew me to her. "How are you holding up? We haven't had any time alone for the last week."

"I'm hanging in there. That studio space near that art gallery is perfect. I get to see the busy streets and hear the bustle of the people below but get to keep the insanity of the city away from me while I work."

"I wish you would have told me you planned to rent it. I would have given it to you for free, considering I owned the building."

I pursed my lips. "Separation of church and state. Business and family are two different things. This is my venture, and if I told you I was interested in the space, you would have lost out on the fair market value."

"You're my sister."

"Ditto. And you are carrying my nephew. He has to eat."

Eva shook her head and rubbed her growing belly. "This kid is heir to a billion-dollar fortune. I think he'll have plenty of food."

The doors of the church dressing room opened, and Leo and Lucian strode in as if they hadn't a care in the world.

They scanned everyone in the room, shot each other a glance, and homed in on Eva.

"Ready to make an honest man out of Finn Hughes?" Lucian asked, which immediately brought a gasp from Mom's lips.

"Really, Lucian. What if someone hears you speaking like that? Why draw attention to Eva's condition?"

Leo rolled his eyes. "If people are blind to her upcoming motherhood, they need a punch to the face."

"Can we all pretend to be civilized for one

evening? I have no idea where I went wrong with all of you." Mother lifted her face to the sky as if praying.

Eva covered my mouth as a retort bubbled up, making me scowl at her.

"Are we ready?" Eva asked Mom, who now beamed at her. "Will you walk with me until we reach Dad? And then you can take your seat."

"Of course, my dear. I'm so glad you understand some decorum, even if you skipped the step of waiting until after marriage to bring forth my grandchild."

Ignoring the last part of Mom's statement, Eva offered Mom her hand, and she stepped toward her.

Eva's skills at managing our parents always amazed me. Her finesse and calm skipped me.

We made our way toward the church's vestibule, where all of Eva's bridesmaids waited for us, including my other sister, Daphne, and sisters-in-law, Elaine and Haley.

The wedding coordinator moved everyone into position, not even flinching when Dad grumbled at her about bossing him around, and then the doors opened.

Immediately, my eyes landed on Damon's, and my stomach plummeted.

He was the last person on earth I wanted to see.

Why the fuck was he here?

I'd spent too many hours building my walls to let him hurt me anymore.

His penetrating gaze bore into mine—the intensity, the pain, the need shot straight into me.

Not here, not now. I refused to let Damon see the husk he'd left behind with his betrayal.

Hardening my resolve, I stared past him toward where Finn waited at the altar. Love and adoration shone in his eyes as he strained for a glimpse of Eva.

There, that was love. Unquestioning, desperate, authentic kind of love. The type I deserved. I wouldn't settle for anything less, ever again.

Screw Damon Pierce and his demons for destroying any chance of the happiness we could have found together.

The music from the organs began a smooth melody, indicating the start of the procession. I shifted my shoulders back and waited for my cue to move.

CHAPTER THREE

Damon

"TAKE A SEAT. Someone will bring him out shortly."

I nodded my acknowledgment to the corrections officer and took my position behind the partitioned plexiglass.

Every time I came here, it took all of my will not to sneer at the overpowering scent of pine cleaner, failing to mask the smell of sweat and desperation. Then again, this was the best a maximum-security state penitentiary could do with a slashed budget. The wardens needed every dime they had to keep the inmates sealed inside. They couldn't give a rat's ass where or not if anything did not smell fresh as daisies.

A flash of seeing Sophia in a facility like this popped into my mind, making me clench my teeth. I'd protected her from the hell of this place, but not me.

I gripped the back of my head. Going to the

damn wedding had been a mistake.

Then again, after that fucking intervention, invasion, whatever the hell the two elder Morellis wanted to call it was, I had no choice but to go.

The beauty of Sophia as she walked down the aisle in her silver gown had taken my breath away. Outside of that moment when our eyes had connected when the vestibule doors opened, she'd refused to give me any of her attention.

Cutting me out of her life was for the best, but it hurt no less. She deserved more than I could give her. She deserved better, not someone plagued by memories or a past he barely acknowledged.

The sound of a security alarm alerted me to a prisoner arriving, and I readied for the standard song-and-dance interaction the useless son of a bitch demanded as attention every fucking time we met.

A heavy metal door pushed open, and a white-haired man with a build similar to mine stepped out. Even at eighty-two, Stuart Butler Pierce should look frail and fragile. However, my grandfather was more on the formidable side.

He seemed to thrive in prison as well as he'd done sleeping on thousand thread count sheets in his fifty-million-dollar penthouse in Manhattan.

He'd perfected the game of "Fake it 'til you make it."

Except, I could see through his bullshit. I was his grandson, after all.

In those green eyes that were exactly like mine. He felt the need, the desire, the craving for control. He wanted to lord his power over others. His dream of stepping behind the helm of the empire he built would never come to fruition.

My siblings, Claire and Sean, made sure of it when we sold the company piece by piece. They found closure when we finalized the papers, and the money hit our accounts, vowing never to have anything to do with our grandfather again.

Then again, neither of them was ever burdened with being the oldest or one compared to the ever-hated grandfather and father.

Then there was the fact this jackass was the last of our elder relatives.

Jesus. Why was I here again?

Oh yeah. Guilt and obligations of being Stuart's only relative willing to give him the fucking time of day.

A smirk touched his lips as he sat on the other side of the partition. Would he greet me like a civilized person and jump right to insults?

I pushed the button to open up the two-way speaker.

Before I could say a word, he spoke in words tinged with an Irish accent. "You look like hammered shit. Is the supermodel not putting out for you?"

Insults it was.

"Good to see you too, Grandfather." I lifted my wrist, looked down at my watch, noted the time, and spoke. "You have your required ten minutes per our agreement. Tell me whatever it is you need me to hear."

"You think you're something big with your degrees and money. Remember, I'm the one who got you there."

I inclined my head. "Noted."

"Everything you have is because of what I brought over from my homeland. The money, the power started with me."

Here it started. The same song and dance. He needed to show me he was the boss, even behind bars or plexiglass.

He wasn't too tired for this shit, but I was. He liked to paint himself as some great patriarch. I refused to let him rewrite history.

What he'd done to begin our family was tainted from the very beginning.

Manipulative bastard, my great grandfather on my grandmother's side had called him, and I couldn't have agreed more. But then again, it was his daughter this fucker had trapped into marriage.

"Everything you had was because you impregnated the fourteen-year-old daughter of an American land baron while he was on vacation with his family in Ireland."

"Your grandmother knew what she was doing."

I kept my face impassive. "Seriously, I'm not in the mood to rehash this story. You have your version. I have the truth. It's getting old."

"What do you know of the truth? I was there, boy."

"As were the many others who gave very different accounts of the story."

"I didn't rape her." The vehemence in his words to cover up his lie always made bile rise in the back of my throat to think I shared genetics with this man.

"Of course, you didn't."

No matter how many times he pretended it away, the truth was the truth. A girl only two days past her fourteenth birthday, who lived a very sheltered life, would never have consented to sex with a total stranger. Much less allow him to lock her in a hotel room without her chaperone for hours.

"She was my wife. Fucking a man's wife is not rape." His voice grew loud and harsh.

I blew out a bored breath. "Let's just state the facts and move on. You were twenty-one, from a different social class and standing. Grandmother Josephine was a child, a virgin without any knowledge about anything. Neither of you would have encountered each other if you hadn't arranged it. You forced yourself on her and compromised her for future marriage prospects. When she discovered she was pregnant, her religious father resounded himself to you as his son-in-law. You got yourself a wealthy prize. End of story."

"You will not disrespect me. I am still the head of our family."

"Who is in this family? Everyone has washed their hands of you. Has Claire or Sean ever visited you, much less acknowledged you, since dear old dad's death?"

My sister and brother refused to give anyone on the Pierce side of the family the time of day. The only exception was our Grandmother Josephine. Then, once she passed away, they cut off ties completely.

Our mother and grandmother were the only people ever to show us any form of love, and this fucker and his look-alike son, David, abused and neglected the purity of the two women until they were husks of the people they were in their youth.

"I know you hate me as much as they do. Why are you here?"

"Because I keep my promises."

He scoffed. "What bullshit. As if you're the type to keep a promise like that."

He wouldn't know anything about honor or keeping promises. No matter how much he'd hurt my grandmother, she'd made me promise to visit him, even if it was for ten minutes.

The man fucking cheated on his wife and then murdered his mistress, and my grandmother wanted me to visit this bastard in jail.

Grandmother Josephine represented everything pure, kind, and loving in the world. Still, no matter how hard she'd tried, she couldn't stop this jackass from turning her son into a twisted version of himself.

She once told me the reason she stepped between my parents, as much as possible, when my asshole father tried to beat my mom was that she had to pay her penance to God for being a bad mother.

She never stopped blaming herself for all the suffering the man currently before me and, in turn, his son caused to the people she loved.

Yeah, they were alcoholics, but even when they were sober, the pair weren't much better.

"Okay, I'll bite. What do you know about me?"

"I know you are just like me and David."

I resisted the urge to grit my teeth. "Why don't you elaborate on this observation."

"Tell me you don't feel it. To put them in their places, make them heed, and show them who's boss."

"You can't bait me."

"I already have." His eyes crinkled at the corner. "I know all about that club with the membership-only access. You go there to get it out of your system. Just because they sign a paper saying you can beat them and fuck them doesn't make you any different from me and your Pa. Don't ever forget it."

The bastard wanted to make me believe my need for domination had anything to do with him and the violence I'd grown up around. Sick fuck. He took pleasure in the idea.

"You know nothing about my club."

"I know you go there to satisfy your rage. You whip them, watch them cry, make them beg. You're as violent as the rest of the Pierce men. It's in the blood, face it."

His words felt as if he had punched me in the gut.

"Only someone like you would twist something consensual between a couple into a vile thing to fit your narrative."

"Is that so? Then why do people at your club call you dangerous?"

I stared at him. Fucking Stuart and his connections.

"And?"

"So you don't deny it."

"That I'm dangerous? It depends on the situation."

"Rumors say you killed your woman." He waved his hand. "Not the model, the other one. Guess she talked back too much, and you got tired of it."

So he knew about Maria. Good for him. With how her brother made the scene at the opening of the new building I constructed not so long ago, it wasn't a real surprise that the news would travel throughout the various circles.

"Why the interest in my personal life? What's in it for you?"

"Nothing. Except for the pleasure of seeing you show your true colors." He snorted.

"You like to justify your choices and project onto others. I'm not you."

"Still resisting, I see. Eventually, you'll end up in the same position I am in. Then you'll have no choice but to admit I was right."

"You and I are nothing alike."

"Stop lying to yourself. You beat women behind the guise of a club. At least I have the balls to do it in the open."

He knew nothing about the world of kink, of the beauty of submission, how power exchange worked. He twisted his mind with lies and rage and expected everyone to fall in line with his beliefs. It was all about control and winning at any cost, and if it didn't work out, he would use his fist.

The last thing I would do was hurt the woman I professed to love in the fashion he used on my grandmother.

Nausea churned in my gut.

Eva was right.

I never gave Sophia enough credit to know what she wanted. I fucking underestimated her at every turn and, in the end, took her choices from her.

I was an idiot, just like my grandfather and father.

My watch beeped, indicating the end of the ten minutes, and I shifted to stand. "Your time is up. Stimulating conversation as always."

"No response to my words."

"I have plenty to say, but there is no point schooling those who lack the discipline to learn."

"School me then."

I stared him in the eyes. "I can guarantee what you and I do are vastly different. You lose control and hurt the people you profess to love. You leave them broken and damaged. I use all my control and restraint to keep my woman on the edge of pleasure. She begs me for the kiss of the whip. She knows only my hand will make her come the way she craves. I build her up and leave her satisfied and smiling."

"That's a fairy tale you paint."

"No. It's a reality selfish men like you can't obtain. We are nothing alike, old man. Let's make it six weeks until our next interaction. We went over your time limit. That should count for something."

Instead of waiting for him to say anything else, I left the room.

CHAPTER FOUR

Sophia

"THIS LOOKS LIKE shit. I thought you had talent," Oliana Dominik voiced her unwanted opinion in a heavy Russian accent as she strode through my studio a little before ten in the evening.

"I didn't ask for a critique, so get lost." Then I frowned, taking in the six-foot-tall blonde Russian mobster's wife dressed in a skintight silver catsuit and white coat. "How the fuck did you find me here? No one is supposed to know the location of my studio."

Oliana rolled her eyes. "We're friends now. I know everything about you."

"But are we? Last I thought, you just stalked me all over the place." I lifted my fingers as I sat behind my drafting table. "First, it was the warm and welcoming jail cell."

She gave a dramatic hug to her heart. "Yes, when Nikki tried to convince me to give him a baby."

"You stabbed him in the balls with an earring." I pursed my lips.

"Yes. Yes, I did." She shook her head. "No more babies."

"Then you showed up at the shelter no one is supposed to know about." I cocked a hand on my hip and stood. "Now you're here. How the fuck did you get past my security?"

She shrugged her shoulders. "Child spy, remember? I know things. The training remains even if I don't play anymore. Well, unless someone messes with my Nikki. Then I break them."

"Yeah, I know. The only one allowed to mess with Nikki is you."

She smiled. "Exactly."

"Now tell me what you want. I'm busy."

"I want to be your assistant."

I covered my hands over my face and lifted it to the ceiling. "Mother Mary, I promise to be a good girl from this day forward if you save me from this."

"Too late, I've already volunteered. You don't need to pay me or anything. I only want to learn." She moved to a dress form with a half-draped piece, fingered some pleats, traced the corset, and nodded. "And I want to be the one to model this one."

Well, it looked as if I had my model with the attitude.

"Figures. It's called My Mistress."

Oliana clapped her hands. "Okay, what can I do?"

"You're fucking kidding me, right?" I gaped at her. "You're serious about working with me and helping me with my new collection. This is all shit work. Like, cutting fabric and the crap we did at the shelter stuff."

"What, you don't think I can do hard work?" Oliana jerked her chin out, giving me an offended glare, and then unbuttoned and threw a coat worth at least ten grand on the floor behind her.

"I'm not sure you can take not being the boss. In here, I'm in charge. You don't have any say. Got it?"

"No opinions?"

"No. My collection. My design. No one gets credit but me."

"I'm not here to steal your designs."

"Cut it with the offended crap. I'm just setting expectations. Even if I'm the stupidest person in the world, I feel like I can trust you, so I'm allowing you into my circle. I don't care if you're some crazy bitch assassin if you fuck me over, I will haunt you."

"I would never betray family. We're family, Sophia."

Wait, was that hurt on her face at me thinking she'd stab me in the back?

Being around this woman confused the hell out of me.

"Explain to me when we became related."

"The moment you protected my niece from Randolph. You took her to your home, comforted and gave her security to keep her safe. That is what family does. We are family now. There is no getting rid of me."

"Umm, does Nikki know this, considering I'm a Morelli?"

She nodded. "Nikki reached out to your brother. They are allies now. Everything is beautiful."

"Oliana, you bulldoze over everyone, and people have no idea how they ended up giving you what you wanted."

"I am who I am." She motioned with her chin. "I want to learn. Put me to work."

"Okay, you asked for it. I need all the fabrics sorted into the bins based on color hues. Once you finish that, we will have enough space to lay out the comparison sketches. I'm having trouble deciding on the base for the centerpiece of the collection. Maybe everything out in the open will clear it up."

"Did you say you want me to sort fabrics?" She eyed the half-opened boxes overflowing with bolts of the various materials I ordered for the project.

"In all of what I said, you caught only the manual labor part?"

Oliana looked down at her manicured nails and sighed. "Fine. Fine. Nikki owes me a massage tonight. Let me go get changed into something comfortable."

"You sneaky bitch. You planned this and came prepared."

"One day soon, my antics won't surprise you. Show me where to change. My girl Nata is bringing up my clothes."

"Don't make me regret this."

✧ ✧ ✧

A LITTLE BEFORE midnight, I stretched my arms above my head, leaned back on the floor where Oliana and I sat, and yawned. "Want to call it a night? I hate to say this, but I do enjoy your company, even if you are a crazy bitch."

"We are both the same. You only pretend to

be a good girl." Oliana stared up at the loft ceiling as she lay on her back.

Gone was her catsuit and expensive coat, and in its place was a coordinating pair of jogging pants and a sweatshirt in shades of sage.

A tray with snacks sat between us, along with cups and a coffee carafe.

A serene calmness seemed to have settled over Oliana's features, giving me a glimpse of the woman behind her persona. No matter how much I wanted to deny it, I liked her.

And maybe, just maybe, I needed someone with her attitude in my life. She made me feel less alone, and the fact she kept pushing her way into places made me feel wanted.

Yep, it was official. I was a nutjob.

Having Oliana "voluntold" me that she planned to wear the *My Mistress* outfit technically made things so much easier for me. This meant I tailored one of my signature pieces to the model, and the diva would work the clothes the entire time she walked the runway.

I only hoped Nikki didn't have visions of slitting my throat for the revealing outfit his wife would wear in front of thousands of people. One run-in with a person trying to kill me was more than enough for this lifetime.

I could only imagine how things were going for Carla Justine. With the media attention surrounding the Randolph family and her being a key witness against them, her life was more than likely chaos. My heart ached for her. Yeah, she tried to kill me, but the whole attempt was half-assed at best, according to Lucian.

Carla was just another victim in the long line of Randolph carnage, except she had some sense knocked into her when I punched her in the face, and she decided to change course.

"So, are we leaving or sleeping on the floor?" Oliana asked, breaking into my thoughts.

"You head home. I'm going to crash in the bedroom here. I have a supplier coming early and would rather not fight traffic to make it on time."

Oliana pushed up to sit. "You do look bad. Sleep. Maybe some sex would do you good, too."

"Are you kidding me right now?" I frowned at her. "What happened to Nikki, and I don't share?"

"No. That is not what I meant." The outrage in Oliana's voice had me smiling. "I'm married. Nikki would kill us both."

"So you would fuck me if you were single?"

She smirked. "I'd corrupt you in more ways than you could ever imagine possible."

A tingle shot down my stomach, remembering Damon saying something similar to me.

"Then where do you expect me to have sex?" I rose to my feet, offered Oliana a hand, and pulled her to standing.

I looked at the floor and sighed. Drawings and fabric samples were strewn all over the ground.

I waved my hand. "That will stay there until morning."

"Okay, then I'll be here too."

"Don't you have nightclubs to run and children to raise?"

"I do. But I want to do this more. I take the babies to school and come here."

I cocked a hand on my hip. "What is the real reason you're doing this? The truth."

"You need a friend. I need a friend. Too many fakes. You aren't scared to tell me that I'm a bitch. I know I'm a bitch. I like that."

I swallowed. "Okay. See you tomorrow."

Oliana gathered her belongings and headed in the direction of the elevator.

"Wait. You never answered the sex question. Want to elaborate?"

"Look behind you. There is a man in the kitchen. He's been waiting patiently to talk to you while we were chatting. I'm sure he will service your needs."

"Are you fucking kidding me right now, Oliana?" I turned to find Damon leaning against a wall, watching my interplay with Oliana. "How long have you been spying on us?"

His intense green eyes bore into mine, and my pulse jumped. "Since the two of you were discussing belt materials."

I whipped my head around and glared at Oliana. "That was over twenty minutes ago. He's been in my loft for nearly half an hour, and you said nothing? What kind of spy are you?"

"The kind that wanted your lover to hear our conversation."

"He isn't my lover."

"I'll leave the two of you to sort out your relationship status." She strode to me, kissed me on the cheek, and then waved to Damon before stepping onto the elevator.

"How did you make it past my security when you're on the do not allow in list? And what do you want?"

Instead of answering my questions, he said, "You need to be more aware of your surroundings."

"My personal mafia queen assassin would have

handled it. Now answer the questions."

"Do you understand what it means to become a member of the Dominik circle?"

"Probably better than being part of the Morelli circle. Why are you here, Damon?"

"To apologize."

"And."

"And I know how to navigate around private personnel."

"Fine, let me hear it." I folded my arms across my chest.

"Won't you look at me?"

"No. Get on with it."

I couldn't look at him when I only wished to feel his arms around me again, to calm this chaos around me.

He wasn't who I thought he was. I couldn't depend on him. He wasn't my safe place anymore.

"I'm sorry."

I nodded, released a deep breath, and pointed to the elevator. "You said it. Goodbye, Mr. Pierce."

"Don't you want to know what I'm sorry for?"

I closed my eyes, feeling that pull toward him. I wanted him, needed him, and he'd broken my heart, shattered it into pieces. I refused to live through it again.

"Say it. I'm tired. I want to go to bed."

"I'm sorry for not believing you to know what you wanted, not trusting you to make your decisions. I shouldn't have taken away your choices. I made a lot of mistakes with us. I'm sorry."

"Okay." I swallowed, unsure what else to say, with the war of emotions churning through my body.

I pivoted toward the stairs leading to the open bedroom as if in slow motion.

Damon stepped in my path right when I was about to pass him. "That's it."

"What do you want me to say?"

"Something other than okay."

I refused to lift my gaze to his. The second I broke I'd lose myself to his spell.

"Would you rather I say I don't forgive you?" It took all my effort to keep the quiver of tears from my question.

"It's better than no real response."

"Fine, then let me add." I shoved him in the chest. "You're a fucking coward for not talking to me. I should hate you for what you did."

"But you don't." He grabbed my wrist before

I punched him in the gut.

I clenched my eyes tight, refusing to cry anymore for this man. "I don't know what I feel. Go away."

I wanted to run as far away from this man as possible. I'd worked so hard to overcome all the feelings of rejection and betrayal. I'd started picking up the pieces. Why had he come back? Couldn't he see there was no going back?

I couldn't allow us to go back.

"Look at me, Sophia," the command in his voice awoke the burning deep inside of me, and without thought, my eyes met his emerald ones.

The shock of staring up at him, seeing the emotions, the man up close again tugged at my heart.

He seemed so different and yet the same. The unkempt beard now covered his jaw. It was a look that sharply contrasted with the well-groomed one he usually maintained. And the shadows under his eyes told me he'd slept as little as I had.

Was he thinner?

"You look like shit," I blurted out before I realized what was coming out of my mouth.

"Well, I didn't have you around to keep me in line."

"I don't have that kind of power over you,

Mr. Pierce."

"You're the only woman who has any power over me, ever."

"Not falling for that line." I tugged at the arm in his grasp. "Or anything in that realm."

We'd been in a similar situation to this. Damon had questioned my innocence and broken my trust in him. Then he'd used words to convince me he loved me.

No. My foolish self wanted to believe Damon loved me and projected it upon him.

God, my thoughts were a jumbled mess, and nothing made sense.

Logically, I knew he cared for me, but love. That was the thing I questioned. Was he even capable of it? Especially after he threw what we had away?

"Don't you dare try to convince yourself it was a lie." He pulled me toward him, bringing his face to mine. "I know what you're thinking."

"You know jack shit about me."

"I know you better than anyone else on this goddamned earth." The vehemence in his response gave me the urge to punch him.

"Keep dreaming. I don't even know who I am myself. How the fuck could you know me?" I shoved at him with my free hand, and he spun me, pinning me against the wall. "I hate you. I hate you."

"Do you? Do you really?"

"Yes," I shouted the lie as tears streamed down my cheeks.

He dropped his forehead to mine. "That's too bad. Because I love you. And I'm sorry I didn't give you the words sooner."

"No. You don't get to say it and think everything is better. I won't forgive you."

"I didn't expect you to." He moved closer to me, pressing his firm body to the front of mine, and then glided a palm around my throat, tilting it up and squeezing. "However, it doesn't change a few facts about us."

My heartbeat jumped, loving the press of his fingers against my skin.

How I missed his touch. My nipples immediately responded, and arousal pooled between my legs.

"There is no us," I countered, and his grip tightened, but I wasn't letting him off the hook. "You made sure of it."

"I was wrong. There is no ending us."

"Too late to change your mind. You've done the damage. I don't want you anymore. Get lost."

His palm moved from my throat into my hair,

fisting it into a brutal hold. The intensity of his dark green gaze ignited an ache I'd barely contained over the last weeks.

"You relinquished your hold over me. I'm free to do what I please, with whomever I please. You mean nothing to me anymore."

"I'll make a liar out of you the second I slide my hands down your pants."

"Physically wanting you is vastly different than mentally wanting you."

"Since I'm already halfway to the finish line, I think I'll stay the course." He jerked my head back.

"What the hell does that mean?"

"This." He covered my mouth with his.

CHAPTER FIVE

Damon

WITH AN INSATIABLE drive to gorge on her, I feasted on her lips. She haunted me for the last few weeks, and I had to have her.

When I awoke this morning, the only thing on my mind was to clear the monthly obligation with the old man. Perhaps it was the way my conversation ended with the asshole. Still, somehow, I found myself driving toward this part of the city and near Sophia's studio.

It wasn't until a text from Oliana Dominik's security telling me to take the fire escape to Sophia's loft that I even considered a visit. I guessed I owed the mob queen a favor for her need to play matchmaker.

I hadn't a clue what I'd expected coming here, but losing myself in Sophia's arms was the last thing on my radar.

"Fuck," I groaned as Sophia scored her teeth across my lower lip and then bit down, leaving me no doubt she'd drawn blood.

Pulling back, I saw the fire lit in her dark, onyx eyes. "It's not going to be that easy for you. You have to work for it."

"Is that right?" I narrowed my gaze and licked at the corner of my mouth, confirming her vicious attack. "Is that the game we're playing?"

"This isn't a game, Damon."

"Yes, it is. You just don't like the rules."

She tried to shove me off her, but it only trapped her arm between our bodies. "An orgasm isn't worth this. I'd rather go to bed."

"Has it ever been just one orgasm? By my count, I've given you two or three on the lower end each time."

She glowered at me. "Wrong. You've fucked me and left me with none. Did you conveniently forget those times?"

"I did make up for it so that I would put those infractions in the void column."

"No on my account. You're in the hole with me. And it will take you a long time to dig your way out of this grave."

"I told you I love you. Does that count for anything?"

She swallowed, and a flash of pain passed through her eyes. "I needed you to say it and trust in it a while ago. But you didn't."

I hated every ounce of anguish I caused her. She deserved so much better than me, but I couldn't let her go.

"I'll make it up to you."

"I don't believe you."

"You will."

"Why won't you take no for an answer."

"You haven't once said no."

She stared at me. "You confuse me to the point I go against my better judgment. You aren't good for me."

"But you can't resist me." I tugged her flush against me.

"I just can't. You fucking better make this worth it." She met my lips halfway, and her arms crept up and encircled my neck.

I lifted her by her thighs, wrapping them around my waist, and carried her up the stairs to the open loft bedroom.

There was only a mattress on the floor, surrounded by clothes of all types. Many of them were in various stages of design, and others hung on racks. The clothing all had an edge of inspiration from things worn by the patrons of Violent Delights.

She caught me studying the garments. "None

of this has anything to do with you."

"Of course, it doesn't," I responded, returning my attention to her.

Emotions swirled in her eyes, and I knew it had something to do with me. Or at least partially to do with me.

She stepped into the world of Violent Delights on her own, but I was the one who brought out the sensuality in her. She chose me to open up her box of possibilities, her unknowns. Everything she knew was because of me.

I slid her down my body and then walked her backward toward the bed, or what there was of the bed.

Goose bumps prickled her skin as the flush on her cheeks deepened. "What do you plan to do to me?"

The words I wanted to say went along the lines of pushing her to her knees and making her deep throat my cock, but instead, I asked, "What do you want me to do you?"

"This is your game. I'm merely a participant. I don't even know the rules."

I gathered the edge of her shirt and lifted it over her head to reveal her black lace bra and her straining nipples, peeking through the lace.

"Sophia, Sophia, Sophia, always the brat."

"I'm never going to change Damon. You're in trouble if you're not used to it now."

"I was in trouble the instant our eyes connected in the club." A crease formed between her brows, and immediately, I ran a thumb over it. "That doesn't mean I want you to change. There is no end to us."

"You keep saying that, but did we ever really start, or was it all an illusion?"

I narrowed my gaze at her. "What do you mean by that? Do you think I would've gone to the lengths I have for anybody but you?"

"What am I to you, Damon? I know I'm the worst submissive on the planet. I don't fit into your box. I don't do as you expect. I'm not like your perfect women of the past."

I resisted the urge to clench my teeth. She was the only perfection I'd ever encountered.

"You're going to push this, aren't you?"

"Oh, I fucking am. I'm not going to give an inch. I want to know what I am to you."

"You're mine."

"And what exactly does that mean?" Anger entered her eyes, and she crept backward. "You keep saying that, but I have no clue what it means. All you do is confuse me. I need more than statements. I need to understand."

"It means I love you, and I'm not letting you go."

"You say you love me, but until twenty minutes ago, you never spoke the words. Plus, why should I believe you after what happened at the club?"

"You keep saying you're not playing a game. But it looks like you are."

I stalked her until her heels hit the mattress, and she stumbled back, grabbing my shoulders. However, I caught her around the waist right before she fell.

Setting a knee on the mattress, I lowered her onto the duvet and then caged her with my body.

Her dark eyes burned up into mine. "I want answers."

"You're not getting them. Not at the moment, anyway." I brought my nose a hairsbreadth from hers. "Submit."

"No." Her nails dug into the back of my neck, and I grabbed hold of them and pinned them above her head.

Her pupils immediately dilated, and her lips parted, taking shallow breaths. My cock responded, wanting to fuck her until she admitted what she refused to acknowledge.

"Submit, Sophia."

She clenched her jaw. "Not happening."

"I know what you're doing, Sophia. I see it in your eyes. I will follow through."

"What is it that you think I want? What is it that The Great Damon Pierce sees?"

"You want me to force you into this? You want me to make you submit, punish you, take that control from you. You've been feeling out of control, Sophia. Tell me I'm wrong."

"Don't psychoanalyze me, Damon." The sharp bite to her words emphasized how I understood the root of her turmoil.

"Then what do you want me to do?"

She could hide from everyone but me. I saw her.

And for some fucking reason, she saw me.

"Either make me come or get out."

I couldn't help but smile at her. Even pinned under me, she wasn't going to give me an inch.

"We both know I'm not leaving."

"Then get to it."

I looked around me and found a box with what looked to be yards of three-inch wide spools of silk in an array of colors, sitting under a mannequin with what looked to be a form with a half-constructed corseted gown.

Interesting.

"Do you ever model your pieces while you create?" Using the heel of my shoe, I tugged the box in my direction.

"Not usually." She gave me a weary glare. "I'm not sure I like that look in your eyes."

"You're the one who said it was my game with my rules."

"Meaning."

Her uncertainty had me smiling. With me, she couldn't hide behind the mask of Sophia Morelli for very long. I made her feel too much, want too much, need too much.

If I could only make her believe it was the same way for me in reverse. But I'd fucked up, and now I'd pay the price.

Slowly, I'd make the sacrifice even if it meant I paid my penance in blood.

"You're going to watch while I turn you into a masterpiece, and then I'm going to fuck you."

Her attention shifted to the box. "With those?"

"What's wrong with them?"

She frowned and then sighed. "I rejected that design after spending too much time and money on all the buttery silks. I wanted it to be the centerpiece of the collection, but in the end, it turned out to be a dud."

"Then I'll use your leftovers to make you into my masterpiece."

Her mouth curved up at the corner. "Are you planning to give me a run for my money in the fashion industry?"

"Something like that." I kissed her forehead and tugged her to stand, turning her to face a full-length mirror with her back to my front.

My body dwarfed hers, all but engulfing it in size. But something had changed about Sophia. There seemed to be an aura of fragility around her that wasn't there before, making her seem even more delicate and precious.

However, on top of it all sat that iron will of hers, determined to build the walls of her defenses to keep me and everyone out.

I planned to break down those barriers even if it killed me.

Holding her gaze in the reflection, I undressed her. First, I removed her shoes and socks, then her linen pants. I continued until I had her completely naked.

Her body was a work of art, especially her full hips and breasts. She modeled on the runways but with an atypical body type. There was nothing overly skinny about her. I wanted to feast on her, gorge on her, lock her away in my penthouse, and keep her all to myself. But she was no longer mine.

Soon. Fucking soon. That would change. By the end of the night, soon.

"Are you going to join me in this nude exhibition?" She licked her lips and then ran a finger down the center of her breasts in a teasing caress meant to entice.

"Eventually. The second I strip. I'll want to bury myself deep inside you. So we'll hold off on that for now." Then, before I could stop myself, I stupidly asked a question I already knew the answer to, "Do you trust me?"

The humor disappeared from her eyes, and she shook her head. "No."

The speed with which she answered felt as if she had shot me in the heart.

No matter how much I expected and deserved the response. It gutted me.

I'd earn her forgiveness. That was my vow.

She turned, desire and determination etched on her beautiful face. "Let me rephrase. With my body, there is no one else I will ever give myself completely. Even if what happened at the club says otherwise, I know you. But when it comes to my heart. Not in the least."

"I suppose I deserve that." We stared at each

other, the pulse of so many things unsaid between us. "You will forgive me one day."

"That's a bold statement. Are you so sure of that?"

I settled my palms at her waist and then up her taut stomach to cup her breasts. "Absolutely."

She arched into my hold and then gasped when I pinched her nipples.

"Arrogant as always."

I repositioned her to face the mirror, scanned the variety of colors in the box, and then decided on the white spool of silk. It wasn't truly white, more on the ivory side, and something that would look exquisite on her light golden skin tone.

"Let's see what I can do with this on you."

"Didn't we already do the tying up thing before?" she asked, referring to the encounter we'd had in the fabric room of a fashion school not so long ago.

"I don't plan to restrain you, so this experience is completely new. Plus, the sensations of silk versus rope are vastly different." I uncoiled some of the silk and teased the delicate column of her neck with the tip of the material. "Want to try it?"

She spread her arms out, smirking, and said, "I'm game."

Moving in front of her, I lifted her hair and

brought the silk ribbons around her shoulders, setting it on her collar like a tie. Then, I began to work a crisscross shape over and around her chest and breasts. With each pass off the spool, I cinched and compressed her skin and muscles, restricting her breathing. I used no knots as I had with the ropes in the fabric room of the fashion school. This was more of a weave from her shoulders, down her breasts, and along her abdomen and torso.

Her nipples puckered and strained as the blood flowed to the tips, begging for attention. With the white silk, I created an intricate corset around her body, accentuating her sensual perfection.

She kept her eyes on me, head slightly tilted back, not saying a word. Only the shallow pants of her breath and the slight shifts of her legs gave away the heightening of her arousal.

Deciding to add to her desire, I picked up another spool, this one in a shade of light pink. I cut a small section, took the strip, and covered her eyes, tying the fabric behind her head.

"Damon," she gasped, her palms resting on my chest.

"From now on, all I want you to do is feel. I promise I'll make it worth your while."

She swallowed. "I hope you do."

"It's a promise." I leaned down, taking her lower lip into my mouth and giving it a bite, hard enough to sting but not break the skin.

I moved behind her to create a binding that added an extra constriction but still allowed her to breathe, even if it was with some restrictions.

Her skin flushed, and her lips parted as a whimper escaped.

She clutched her fingers against her palms, and she squeezed her thighs together as she shifted side to side. "Damon, what is happening to me?"

"The real question is, do you like it?"

Goose bumps pebbled over her skin, and she leaned her weight along the front of my body. "Yes."

"What does it feel like?"

"It's different than the ropes, but I feel more confined for some reason, as if I'm more bound to you."

"Is that a good thing or a bad thing?" I slid my fingers down to her exposed slick pussy lips and stroked the tip of her swollen clit peeking out.

"I don't know." She gasped and arched into my touch, grasping my arm. "Please, I need."

"What is it you want?"

She shook her head. "I have no idea. This is so

different. The sensations."

Her confusion had me smiling. I pushed my fingers into her sopping core, pumping in and out of her. Her muscles contracted around me, flooding me with her desire. Her legs grew weak, and I circled my arm around her waist to hold her up, continuing my ministration.

Bringing her right to the point of going over, I stopped, pulling out of her heat; I brought my fingers to her lips. "Suck."

She followed my command, licking up her essence.

I walked her forward, closer to the full-length mirror. Pulling the mask off her eyes, I let her adjust to the light in the room and made her look at herself, her arousal coating her mouth, her glazed eyes, her exquisite swollen pussy lips, wet and glistening.

Her gaze met mine. Her hunger in her eyes was so raw my cock grew to a steel rod, heavy and so ready to fuck.

"Are you going to leave me hanging?"

"Do you think I would leave you hanging after not having you for so many weeks?"

"You do have a sadistic side."

I fisted her hair and jerked her head back. "You only see that part of me when your brat side goes too far."

"Admit it. You love that side."

She had no fucking idea how much the things I never would have accepted before her were the things I couldn't get enough of from her. It felt like I lived a half-existence without her smart mouth or attitude. Her unique vitality brought something into my life that I never knew was missing. It confused me on so many levels and, at the same time, grounded me in a way I never knew I needed.

I brought her mouth to mine, drinking in her intoxicating taste, and then muttered against her mouth, "You're vital to me, Sophia."

"Don't say things like that. I might just believe you."

My fingers tightened against her scalp. "Meaning?"

"I won't let you hurt me again."

"That's the plan."

"We'll see." She studied me in the reflection and cocked her head to the side. "Are you going to fuck me or talk?"

"Have it your way." I pushed her to the floor.

The corset I'd weaved around her accentuated her hourglass figure, and the way she sat back on her heels without me telling her gave me pleasure in a way she wouldn't understand.

"Why are you staring at me like that?"

"You please me."

"I make you crazy."

"That too." I cupped her cheek, unable to help myself, and then ran my thumb over her lips. "Keep your eyes on the mirror."

She nodded her acknowledgment and watched me as I stripped. Her eyes dilated while taking in everything about me. The intensity of her stare aroused me on a different level. Until her, the adoration of women wasn't something I ever focused on. I knew my appeal; I understood what I had to offer.

With Sophia, her desire for me, her need, her craving, went straight to my soul. It brought out a possessiveness, unlike anything I'd ever felt before.

She licked her lips the moment my cock came into view. She focused on the stroke of my hand, pumping up and down as I kneeled behind her.

Her lips parted, and her breathing grew ragged. "Damon, why do you make me wait?"

"The anticipation gets you off. We both know this." I wrapped an arm around her waist and drew her to my front, my hard cock a thick brand along her bare behind.

A whimper escaped her lips as she ground

against me.

"The white makes you look almost innocent," I told her, studying our reflections. "However, we know there is nothing innocent left about you."

I pushed her forward, forcing her to catch herself with her arms, and in the next moment, I drove into her, thrusting balls deep.

"Oh, God," she cried out, her head thrown back and the arch of her spine with the silk binding making her appear as if she were one of those photographs from the club come to life.

Her pussy muscles squeezed around me, fluttering and quivering, and I closed my eyes, loving the exquisite feel of her.

She was absolutely perfect.

I gripped her hips and set a slow, steady pace, wanting to revel in finally having her again.

"Harder, will you stop teasing me? Make me come. You owe me."

Of course, the brat refused to give in, even for a few seconds.

I came over her and caged her with my body, all the while continuing my measured rhythm.

"You're very bossy, Sophia. But you forget," I rolled my hips, pushing her closer to the release she craved. "I'm the Dom. You get what I give you."

"Then give me an orgasm."

I slid a palm down her silk-covered torso and to her swollen clit, sliding it between my knuckles. At the same time that I pinched the sensitive flesh, I pulled my cock out to the hilt and slammed into her pussy.

"Damon," she screamed, clamping down around me like a vise grip, her head thrashing and her eyes clenched tight.

She rode out her release with gasps and incoherent babble, then when she finally came down, she murmured, "I want more."

"You're greedy."

She tilted her head to glance over her shoulder. "It is all that I trust you to give me now."

I clenched my teeth. Pulling out of Sophia's clenching pussy, I flipped her to her back and loomed over her.

"Is that how you truly feel?"

She took in shallow inhales, a combination of the exertion of the sex and the restrictive bindings. "Yes."

Spreading her thighs, I pushed into her. If that's how she wanted it. I'd give it to her.

"I will fuck you all night long. You asked for it."

She narrowed her eyes, lifting onto her elbows

and bringing her face to mine. "Go right ahead. Like I said. You owe me."

I owed her for a lot of things, but this attitude of hers pissed me off.

Fisting her hair, I covered her mouth with mine and began to fuck her the way she wanted, hard and relentless. Every damn part of her would ache by the time morning came.

And then she'd have to face one significant consequence of this night, the fact she was no longer on birth control.

CHAPTER SIX

Sophia

I STIRRED FROM a heavy sleep as the sound of running water in the bathroom downstairs reached my ears. I opened my eyes. Darkness still encased the loft, telling me it was long before dawn.

Stretching my arms above my head, I winced and then moaned at the ache in my muscles, especially between my legs.

Jesus. How many times had Damon fucked me last night?

It was as if every time I dozed off, he woke me with his mouth or cock.

Okay, I had dared him in a sense to prove he could do it, but I never actually expected him to do it.

Note to self: never dare Damon Pierce to do anything.

No matter if he'd proven himself a sex god or whatever. My physical need for him wasn't going to wash away the pain he'd caused me.

The weeks apart from Damon had taught me one thing—telling myself I was worth more than the scraps he'd thrown my way and actually believing it or acting like it were completely different things.

I refused to go backward. I knew my value. If Damon wanted me, he had to work for it.

He could fuck me until his dick fell off, but I had no plans to change my mind.

Shifting, I winced. There was no chance of his dick falling off with the way we went at it. My tender pussy, on the other hand, would require an icepack STAT.

Rising from the mattress, I mindlessly searched for the switch to the lamp. Once I found it, I turned on the light and took a survey of the mess Damon and I had made of the bedroom area of the loft.

Fabrics of all types lay all over the place, along with pieces of white silk ribbons. If Damon's goal was to fuck me on every available surface up here, he definitely managed it.

How was I going to explain any of this to the vendors who were coming here today?

I couldn't help but groan as I realized the person responsible for cleaning up the mess was me.

I'd tackle all this once my brain could function and focus on something other than my aching nether region and lack of caffeine. Number one on my to-do list was coffee.

I found my robe hanging from a wall, slipped it on, and then made my way to the kitchen on the lower level of the studio.

Just as I pressed the button on my grinder, Damon stepped out of the bathroom with a billow of steam behind him. His emerald eyes scanned me in that predatory way of his, sending a shiver down my spine.

No matter how much my brain wanted to resist him, my insatiable desire for him seemed to take hold whenever he was anywhere near me. Even my abused pussy was ready for action, knowing her dumbass would pay the price later.

Small beads of water dotted his shoulders, and his skin held the glow from the hot shower, making my fingers itch to touch him.

I bit the inside of my cheek, trying to ignore the slow humming of the desire growing deep in my core.

"I expected you to be still sleeping."

"I rarely sleep in. You know this." I shifted my attention to the water kettle, filled it, and set it on the warming plate. "I'm making coffee. Want some?"

"Yes."

I pulled out two mugs and set them on the counter.

"I also know you need a minimum of five hours sleep, or you're piss and vinegar. And since you are leaning toward the latter side, what is wrong?"

"Nothing is wrong. I have things on my mind."

"As in?"

You, this thing called love, and figuring out what I'm doing with my life.

Instead of saying my honest thoughts, I said, "My collection and my plans for the future."

"So that means us."

"Does it?" I asked, lifting my gaze to his. "I wasn't aware that an 'us' existed."

He furrowed his brow and prowled in my direction, but I remained still, not letting him intimidate me with his presence. "Last night, there definitely was an us."

"Is that so? Who made this decision?" I cocked a hand on my hip.

"You made that decision long ago."

"Did I? Want to remind me when I decided this? Because as far as I know. We aren't together."

"It happened when you walked into that greenhouse and allowed me to claim you. I warned you to stay away. You decided I was what you wanted. Now you live with the choice."

"It doesn't work that way. You are the one who decided you didn't want me."

"I always fucking wanted you. I took myself out of the picture for you. It was a fucking mistake."

"You can take yourself out again. You don't get to change your mind depending on which way the wind blows." Releasing an exasperated breath, I returned my attention to my coffee. "Besides, I don't recognize your claim, so there is that major fact you need to acknowledge."

I picked up my slow-drip coffee maker, positioned it, and filled the top with grounds before lifting the kettle to pour water over it. As I tipped the container, Damon's hand covered mine, grabbed hold of it, and moved it out of reach.

"What the hell are you doing?" I glowered at him.

His response was to crowd me against the counter, his large body a heated mass towering over me.

"From this moment forward, you and I are a couple. We live together. There is no separation for us. You are mine, Sophia."

"Not a chance." I shook my head and poked him in the stomach. "Listen up, Damon Pierce. All we did was fuck. Get it through your thick head."

I couldn't believe he thought last night meant I'd forgiven him, or that he could order me to move back in, or that we could pretend none of the events of the previous few weeks ever happened.

He lifted me onto the counter, anger and lust glazed his eyes.

"Fucking? You know damn well it's more than you're admitting."

"Since you're such an expert at reading me, why don't you explain it to me."

"It is never only sex with us. What we have goes beyond the physical. We know and love each other. What we have is in a completely different realm than a mere fuck."

"Are you serious? Now that you've accepted your feelings for me, I'm supposed to scramble for every bone you throw my way. Get lost. I have no time for this shit."

"Have it your way. We will have a redo of last night." Before I realized what he meant, he tugged his towel free, jerked my robe open, pulled my legs around his waist, positioned his cock at my slick opening, and slammed in.

"You asshole." Pleasure-filled pain ripped through me, my back bowed, and I scored my nails over his shoulder.

I should hate him for manhandling me like this. But, of course, my damn traitorous body wanted more. Even my over-sensitized pussy wept, wanting everything this man gave me.

"I never denied it. I will fuck you. I will fill you with my cum and then my child. Afterward, you'll have no choice."

"No choice for what? You make no damn sense. We are not a couple. We are not together. And I'm not anything to you."

He withdrew and plowed back in, gritting his teeth with the pistoning of his hips. "You're going to marry me. My children will have my name."

"Keep dreaming, you psychopath." I arched into him, meeting his thrusts, unable to help myself as my body quickened and quivered, ready to satisfy her own selfish needs. "Haven't you learned a damn thing about me? You will never force me into marriage. You'll never force me into anything I don't want to do."

"I still plan to fuck you every chance I get until a part of me grows inside you." He pounded harder, hitting those spots I needed.

My pussy contracted and spasmed. Arousal flooded his cock as my skin tingled with sensation.

"I'm on birth control, you idiot."

He stilled his movements, giving me a calculated smirk. "Are you? You were due for your shot three weeks ago. Have you gotten it?"

I stared into his smug eyes. Was he tracking my cycle?

Then it hit me.

My mind flooded with tidbits of things that happened following my encounter with the makeup artist and my hospital stay. In the weeks of my recovery and even at the club, Damon and I never had actual intercourse. I'd assumed it was all due to my injury, but it was because of the risk of pregnancy. He'd kept up with everything about me when I hadn't.

Anger rose inside me, but for some reason, it heightened my arousal instead of dimming it.

"You're a fucking stalker."

"It was deductive reasoning. You started the shot because of me. If you aren't sexually active, you wouldn't have thought to get the next dose."

"You planned last night."

He clasped my throat in an unyielding hold,

making my breath grow shallow. "No, I didn't. I never intended to come here. It was a last-minute decision."

Bullshit. How the hell does he just come across town to my studio?

"Liar."

"I have never lied to you." The intensity in his green irises showed me the truth of his words, and even though he squeezed tighter, the turmoil bubbling inside me calmed.

"But you don't tell me the truth either."

He clenched his jaw. "I'm working on it."

"Work harder." I dug my heels into his ass. "Finish what you started."

"This conversation isn't over." He withdrew to the tip of his cock and slammed forward, jarring me against the counter.

I set a palm to the backsplash, leveraging my body to help me meet each of his thrusts. "From my point of view, it wasn't a conversation, more of you making demands and me denying you."

"You are a brat." He fisted my hair. "You never fucking listen."

"Well, it still didn't stop you from falling for me or you wanting to lock me away in your ice palace."

"I tried locking you away. You escaped." He

hammered my pussy with hard, measured strokes meant to send me over. "Now I'm on to other methods of binding you to me."

My response caught in my throat as my orgasm washed over me. My body arched as my vaginal walls contracted around Damon's steely length. I thrashed against him while he continued to pound into me, and my core clamped down, flexing and trembling. Sensations cascaded over me, and without thinking, I bit down on his shoulder, so overwhelmed by the fury of the release Damon milked from me.

He kept me suspended, unable to come down as he worked his cock in and out of me, racing toward his own pleasure. His thumb grazed my clit, strumming and circling it, and I flew over again. This time, Damon joined me, pumping hard and hot into me.

He held me close, his face buried against my chest as our breaths calmed.

We remained quiet, neither of us saying a word as if afraid to shatter the intimacy of being together.

The scent of his shampoo teased my nostrils, and I held back a tear as the emotions of all this man had put me through resurfaced from the box I'd worked so hard to stuff them inside.

This time, I refused to make it easy on him.

He wanted me. He'd work for it.

Deciding to break the silence, I said, "I will choose if I'm with you or not. Nothing can bind me to you. Not marriage, not a child. And just so you know, you haven't gotten me pregnant."

"There is no way you can know this." He lifted his head, the firm set of his jaw daring me to challenge his statement.

"I can. I'm due for my period either today or tomorrow. My cycle countered your plans."

"I still want you to move back in with me."

The way he worded it wasn't a command or an order, more in a way of a request, but the meaning was the same. Everything was about his desires and his needs. Yes, mine were there too, but losing him left me in turmoil, and for weeks I had floundered. I couldn't risk it again.

This time, I'd stand on my own two feet first.

"No, that isn't going to happen."

As if hearing my internal monologue, he said, "I'm your Dom. You need the control and the stability I can give you."

I craved those things, wanted those things. I had to remember how Damon had let me down. He hadn't been the Dom I needed. I could only depend on myself to sustain me into the future.

"No, you're not my Dom. I'm not your submissive. That relationship is over." I dropped my head for a second before looking back up at him. "I don't trust you anymore. Especially not after how you pushed me away. We have sex, kinky sex, but it's only sex."

"You can't mean that. You love me."

I shoved him back, forcing him to slip from my body, and jumped off the counter. Shrugging on my robe and tying the belt, I glared at him, my temper roiling up to a boil.

"You arrogant asshole. Are you hearing anything I'm saying?"

"I hear you. You can't forgive me for what I did at the club."

I growled, stalking past him, wanting to throw something hard and lethal at his thick head.

"This isn't just about the damn club. You can't just order me into a relationship, Damon. It doesn't work that way. Love without trust means nothing. Why can't you see that?"

"I'm here telling you I fucked up. I was wrong. What more do you want from me?"

"I want to see all of you, even the parts you think will scare me. You want me to trust you, but you don't trust me. You took my choices from me. It left me feeling like I had no one who believed in me all over again."

"I'm protecting you. You don't want to see those parts of me."

"That's a cop-out. I don't need or want that kind of protection. I've got it handled."

A wave of resignation and exhaustion washed over me.

I walked toward the bathroom and then said over my shoulder. "Until you understand and truly hear me, you can't give me what I want. I have work to do. Goodbye, Damon. Please see your way out."

CHAPTER SEVEN

Damon

A LITTLE BEFORE eleven in the morning, I arrived at a closed construction site for one of my buildout projects in midtown Manhattan. Weather forecasters projected high gale-force winds starting late afternoon as a precursor to a category two hurricane, which was being dubbed a five-hundred-mile-wide superstorm.

Instead of evacuating as most of the sane people in the city should be doing, I was about to start my fourth site visit for the day to ensure my project managers safely and securely shut down all active construction locations.

Then again, considering the amount of traffic I'd just contended with to get here, half of the city had decided to ride out the imminent natural disaster at home.

One thing was always true for New Yorkers. Never tell them what to do. They will always do the opposite. It was their way of saying fuck you to the world.

Putting my car in park, I grabbed my hard hat and sunglasses and stepped out. I gazed up at the first twenty stories of the steel framing of a new high-rise going up. The building would house the corporate headquarters of an aquatics research and engineering firm. Thus, I created a design with angles that gave the illusion of water.

There were still another twenty stories until the framing was complete, but we were ahead of schedule by a month. Which I assumed would make the money men happy.

But, of course, I was wrong. When buildouts came to a grinding halt in New York City, financiers started bitching. It wasn't as if my company was the only one shuttered in preparation for a direct hit from a fucking storm. Still, the investors acted like I made mother-fucking-nature create this cyclone to come toward the city.

Fuckers.

Well, not all of them. Lucian was one of them.

No, he was a fucker too, but on a different level.

He'd roped me into designing this project, and then my idiot self decided to take a cut of the project, so of course, I wanted in on the buildout.

Now I had to deal with fucktards from Palm Beach who knew shit about Big Apple construction.

Another car pulled up behind mine. The make and the model of the sports car told me the driver was the one and only Lucian Morelli.

Not two seconds later, he stepped out of the car, setting a hat on his head. At least he remembered it this time instead of thinking his noggin could withstand a hit with construction debris.

Knowing his visit spelled trouble, I asked, "Why the fuck are you here? Shouldn't you be evacuating with your wife and kids or some shit like that?"

"They left yesterday. I wanted to see if you imploded the building instead of finishing it."

"It was a thought." I stared at the equipment tied down under the tarp before me. "What is the real reason you're here? I have other sites prepped for your specific cleanup necessities."

"I'd use the proper channels for that type of handling."

"Then what's the issue?"

"According to Elaine, you sent Eva ten grand in new mother and baby products after her visit."

It was the least I could do for her. She gave me a perspective on Sophia I hadn't considered.

She'd also shown compassion to me when others would have punched me in the face.

Damn, Morellis were nothing like their reputations.

From what I heard, the gifts arrived just in time. That very evening, Eva went into labor and delivered her little boy. I'd thought about going to the hospital to pay my respects to Eva and meet the new heir to the Hughes empire but decided against it. The chance of running into Sophia and causing her more pain was the last thing I wanted to do.

This time with Eva was something Sophia had looked forward to from the moment I met her. My presence would have only dimmed the joy of the occasion.

"Did you want some baby goods as well?"

"It is common courtesy to show gratitude to all parties involved in caring for an ailing friend.

"I neither asked for nor required your care. Hence, no gratitude. Plus, Eva fed me. You threatened to kill me, bitched at me, and then ate my food. Eva brought me dinner, not you."

"I heated it, so I am allowed to partake."

"Tomato, tomahto. Now, get to your point. I have other sites to visit."

"Is that all you're doing?"

"What the hell does that mean?"

"Where have you been for the last few weeks? I want to know what you're up to. No one sees you around."

"I work. I go home. I work some more. That is my mundane life."

"What does the coveted Dom, Mr. Pierce, do for recreation?"

Was this jackass serious? The thought of touching anyone but Sophia, let alone going to a club, never crossed my mind.

I glared at him. "You think I'm cheating on you and your precious club? Did you forget I'm no longer a member of Violent Delights?"

"I want to know if you're cheating on my sister."

Before I realized I moved, I had Lucian by the collar. "Listen up, Morelli. Sophia and I are a subject you have no part in. Whatever happens between us stays between us."

"You were serious. I never thought I'd see the day," Lucian smirked and chuckled.

"What's so fucking amusing?"

"What you said when you were shitfaced. You can't touch another woman because of Sophia. You're living like a goddamned monk because she's got you by the balls."

I scoured through my memory and then remembered what I'd said to him the morning of his invasion of my penthouse.

I shoved him back. "This is why I don't drink. I fucking get verbal diarrhea."

"What the fuck happened with the two of you? You were supposed to fix it with Sophia?"

"Why don't you ask her?" I gripped the back of my head. "She's your sister."

"She told me to fuck off and mind my own business."

I couldn't help but smile, imagining Lucian's face as Sophia said those words to his face. When she unleashed her Italian temper, it was something to watch. Most people wouldn't dare raise their voice to Lucian Morelli, more on the side of pissing their pants the second he stepped into the room.

"Then you should follow her directive. She means what she says."

I was one to talk.

Especially when I couldn't follow my own advice when it came to Sophia. Then again, she handled me in the same fashion she handled her brother. Well, maybe not in the same fashion, but the message read the same way. It was a loud and clear, fuck off if we planned to boss her around.

"Answer the damn question," Lucian ordered.

"There isn't any way to fix it. She won't compromise on some things, and I can't give them to her. End of story."

"Can't or won't."

"Can't. I don't have the ability."

"Did she say that, or is it you being a pussy?"

"She said it."

"Are you fucking kidding me? That's it. And so you're giving up? Maybe you are a pussy."

"Don't make me punch you in the face, Morelli. I will tie you to one of the pillars and let the storm take you with it." I took a step toward him. "You're a fucking busybody who needs to stay out of my personal life."

That's when I noticed Lucian and my security teams, guns drawn, ready to jump in, and confused as hell, unsure what to do.

I waved my hand at them. "For fuck's sake. We're not going to kill each other. Morelli needs me to clean up his messes too much. Put that shit away."

Lucian nodded, and everyone stood down, holstering their weapons.

"Jesus. I got your panties all twisted. That was fun."

"I'm glad I'm here for your amusement, asshole. Fuck off."

"Fine. I'll let you brood in peace." Lucian turned to head toward his car, but before he moved, he said, "Though it's interesting to see the ice in your veins thawing."

"Want to explain that statement?"

"You're like your buildings, Pierce—all glass and hard steel, cold and unfeeling, like ice. But I got a reaction from you, something I've rarely seen happen. That's Sophia's doing, I'd say. Nice to see you're not a robot."

"Get lost."

Instead of responding, he headed to his car.

Lucian had barely driven off the site when my phone rang.

I pulled out my phone to check the caller ID. The display read the number for the federal penitentiary.

Why the fuck would they be calling me? The last time they'd called, good old grandfather had gotten himself locked in solitary.

I answered, "This is Pierce."

"Are you Stuart Pierce's grandson?" a woman asked.

"Yes. How may I help you?"

"This is Doctor Allen at the FCI Otisville. I want to speak to you about your grandfather."

Okay, this would be interesting. Something about her tone made me believe I wouldn't like what she told me.

The last time I'd received a call like this, he'd gotten in some fight, had his ass handed to him, and ended up in a coma. His ego refused to let him believe the strength of his youth no longer existed.

Instead of walking away when the brother of a cartel boss made some crack at him, his pride got in the way, and he dealt with the consequences.

It was the same fucking reason he ended up in prison in the first place. The need to show one of the women he enjoyed parading around town that she'd heed his word or deal with his wrath.

"Go ahead," I said to Dr. Allen.

"I'm sorry to inform you Mr. Pierce passed away before arriving at the hospital."

Everything inside me froze. I couldn't have heard her correctly.

"Would you repeat that?"

"Your grandfather died about an hour ago. I have you listed as the person of contact for Mr. Pierce."

"Thank you for informing me. Would you mind telling me his cause of death?"

He looked healthy the last time I saw him.

Could he have gotten in another fight?

"He suffered a heart attack during his morning outdoor time."

This seemed too damned convenient and definitely way too easy for the old man's end to come in this fashion. Then again, it would serve him right since all he cared about was his reputation and going down in a blaze of glory.

"I'm sure you know his record. Was it as simple as you're saying, or were other factors involved?"

There was a momentary pause before she spoke, "Are you asking if he was involved in an altercation?"

"Yes. My grandfather isn't the type to keep his opinions to himself. The last time I received one of these calls, he was the loser in a five-against-one fight."

"No. From the reports of the officers on duty, Mr. Pierce spent the morning on the rec field, writing in his journal as he does most days after his meal."

"I see." I couldn't seem to process the reality of the situation. "What now?"

"Claiming of the body and arrangements for his burial. Everything is up to you. The alternative is to leave him with us, and we will assume responsibility for Mr. Pierce's remains."

If only I had the ability to wash away my obligations by handing him over to the State. But no, I'd follow through with this last bit of duty. Then, it would all end forever.

"I will take care of it. Please expect me there in a few hours."

I hung up as a numb haze settled over me. I stared at the construction site with no sadness, hate, or glee at the death of a man who'd created a legacy of so much pain for my family.

I should feel relief to no longer carry the burden of visiting the asshole. I'd fulfilled my promise to Grandmother Josephine.

Instead of that place in my heart where I'd held so much contempt for the bastard, there was nothingness. An empty hole lived there, dark and desolate.

Then, it struck me as if one of the cement towers of the building before me hit my head.

I'd created a prison with thicker walls than the one Stuart lived in for the last fifteen years. One that separated me from everyone around me. I used it as a shield saying it protected others, but I was a fucking liar.

I repeatedly told Sophia I wasn't good enough for her, that I was dangerous, and that she deserved better. Now, she accepted it, but not for the reasons I'd given her. She saw through my bullshit. I wanted all of her without giving her the same in return, and she wasn't having any of it.

The way I remembered her telling me to leave showed me she would let me wallow behind the cell walls I'd created. She was picking herself, her future, even if it meant one without me.

I gripped my hair and lifted my face to the sky.

God, I fucked up so badly, and I had no one to blame but me.

She'd chosen a life without me, and I had to live with the consequences.

CHAPTER EIGHT

Sophia

"WHAT ARE YOU hiding, Sophia?" Oliana demanded as she stepped out of the elevator onto my studio floor. "This working alone thing is annoying. I'm your assistant. Let me assist."

With a mouth full of sewing pins, I lifted my gaze at her and returned my focus to the piece currently on a dress form before me, then mumbled. "A gown."

It was a ruby red cloak with an embroidered hood. Everything about it screamed seduction and indulgence. I'd hoped to make it into the showstopper ensemble. However, as everything came together, this wasn't the one.

I loved it. I even planned to wear it one day when I dared to build up the courage to visit a club again, but this wasn't the design to make my collection. Deep in my gut, I imagined something with binding and silk, a mask, maybe. Perhaps a cloak like this, but not so large or even grander.

I had no idea.

Dear God, I was going to drive myself crazy.

Whatever I created, I wanted it to be the centerpiece of the collection, unique, bold, unexpected.

"Either you tell us what is going on in your mind, or I'm going to hang you upside down from those rafters, and she will help me." Oliana stomped her heeled foot, pointed to the railing above us, and then cocked a hand on her hip.

I noticed Karina mimicking Oliana's stance before I could ask who she brought to assist her.

Oh, for all that was holy.

If I partied too much, someone had an opinion. Now that I worked and stayed focused, these two had issues with it.

I couldn't win for losing.

Pulling the pins from my mouth, I said. "What is this? The Russian and Indian Inquisition?"

"Yes," Oliana and Karina said in unison.

"Locking yourself in the studio isn't healthy. We need you to live a little Sophia. You can't spend every day in this building." Karina stalked up to me and pulled me up from my knees.

The movement had me wincing as a pins and

needles sensation shot through my joints.

Oh, man. That hurt.

Maybe I'd stayed in that position way longer than I'd thought.

"I can't take a break now. I feel it. That final piece. I think it will come to me at any moment."

Karina's face softened. "Look, I get it. I know the obsession to finish a collection when the muse is in overdrive. However, I also know that if you don't take a break, you won't be able to get anything done. You will burn out."

"I'm not burning out. I'm fucking determined. There is a huge difference."

Oliana folded her arms across her body. "You know who's determined? Me. Let's go."

"Where?"

"Wherever I take you." She eyed me from head to toe and curled her nose. "You are not wearing that. Karina, find her some decent clothes. This is a travesty. I thought you were a model with a sense for fashion. I'm burning that as soon as you take it off."

"Look. I get you are all mob queen and push everyone around, but I have things to do, and falling into line when you say jump isn't one of them."

She moved to tower over me. "Don't make

me cut up your designs. I'm the crazy bitch who will do it just to make a point."

I wouldn't put it past the lunatic and her threats to actually go through with them.

"I hate you." I scowled at Oliana.

She shrugged and then smirked. "Maybe right now, but later, you'll kiss and hug me and then tell me you love me."

"I wouldn't hold my breath."

✧ ✧ ✧

"ARE YOU HAVING fun?" Oliana asked as I lounged on plush couches in the VIP section of her newest nightclub, Misha.

I sipped on my sparkling water, gazed at the hordes of bodies packed onto the dancefloor below us, and answered, "No."

Oliana chuckled, ignoring my surly attitude. "You will. I promise."

"That was the guarantee you offered an hour ago. I want a refund."

"So cranky, my darling. Here, have a snack. It will keep you from being hangry." She pushed the charcuterie board my way.

"Cheese and crackers aren't going to make me forget that I'd rather be preparing for my upcoming show."

"There is meat on the plate, too. Don't forget about that. It will help soak up the alcohol." She picked up a cracker, put a piece of cheese on it with some ham, and handed it to me. "Eat."

"If I eat this, will you let me go home?" I took the food from her and popped it into my mouth.

"No. But you can go dancing. I know this is one of your favorite clubs. And since I own the place, you can even live out that diva lie you have everyone believing, and no one will bat an eyelash."

I picked up my sparkling water, drank a few sips, and said, "Does your Nikki enjoy this sense of humor of yours?"

"Sophia, you need to get laid. I don't like this needs servicing side of you." Oliana waved her hand. "You are no fun. Tell her, Karina."

"Don't put me in the middle of this. I helped you get Sophia here. That's where my assistance ends." Karina rose from her seat and leaned on the railing to better view the club's lower level.

"What are you looking at?" I asked, deciding I no longer cared for any more of Oliana's pestering.

"The buffet of inspiration below. People watching sparked the best ideas."

I stepped around Oliana, who glowered at me

and stood beside Karina, setting my forearm on the railing.

I scanned the crowd and all the many styles of club patrons. The clothes were an eclectic mix of the nineteen seventies and eighties fashion mixed with modern trends. The looks weren't about fitting in with each other but more about feeling good in whatever they wanted to wear.

I loved the vibe here. No one cared if you worked as a clerk at the deli down the street or if you starred in the newest Hollywood film.

This club wasn't the type of place found on all the lists of the must-see places of New York City. The only way to garner admission into Misha was to live in the neighborhood or be invited by someone who did.

The fact I'd come to this place three times before this and never knew Oliana owned it, she said this area belonged in her husband, Nickoli Dominik's territory. The people in it were loyal to him and, in turn, her.

My breath caught as my gaze landed on a couple near the bar in the back corner of the room. The woman had jet-black hair and wore a white lace mask over her eyes, which accentuated the deep red hue painted on her plump lips. What made her so striking was the white bustier with the crisscross pattern she wore with her black leather pants. It cinched her waist, giving her that perfect hourglass shape.

Then there was the man behind her, tall, over six feet, with dark blond hair and deep green eyes. He kept his attention on his lady and a possessive hand at her back as they worked their way into the crowd.

My mind drifted to that night Damon spent with me in my studio. My body hummed as the weeks since disappeared. I closed my eyes, remembering how his fingers worked the white silk ribbon all over my body to create the corset-style binding. He'd given me exactly the amount of constriction I craved, needed, wanted.

I'd allowed him to sweep away my resistance with his touch, his presence, his domination.

And briefly, especially as I watched us in the mirror, his body behind mine. I believed we had a future.

But morning came, letting reality seep in.

A tear slipped down my cheek, and I lifted my lashes. Immediately, my gaze landed on the couple's joined left hands, and a burning sensation filled my throat.

They wore wedding bands.

I swallowed, desperate to ease the pain I felt.

Some people attained their happy ending. I wasn't one of them.

No, that wasn't true. I'd find mine, but it would come in an unconventional way.

I took in everything about the pair below me as an unexplainable urge to find a pen and paper surged through me.

Oh, my God. I fucking had it.

I knew what I wanted as my showstopper—the exact look, the exact color, the exact styling, and the model to wear it.

Lizzy.

Turning, I rushed back to the table where a server stood next to Oliana.

"Do you mind if I grab that pen from you and take a few of your napkins?" I asked the pretty brunette, who looked at me as if I was nuts.

She nodded and handed me the items, not saying anything.

I pushed aside the drinks and appetizers, set the napkins before me, and began to draw out the ideas buzzing in my head.

"Are you fucking kidding me right now, Sophia?" Oliana grabbed for my pen, but I dodged her.

"You said a break would help me. Well, it did. I'm inspired. Now let me work."

"Fine. I'm going to find Nikki. He will keep me entertained. You are boring."

"Yes, go. Let him convince you to have another baby."

She stomped her foot. "I said no. He gets no more babies. Five is enough."

I couldn't help but smile as she stalked off with a scowl. I continued to work on the beginnings of my masterpiece with two thoughts running through my head. First, I planned to blow everyone's socks off when I presented this piece. And second, no matter how much I wanted to deny it, Damon was my muse for the collection.

The sensuality, energy, and essence I threw into the creative process came from the emotions I experienced with Damon. Meeting him opened up a doorway inside of me, and I couldn't lie to myself and say it wasn't worth it, even after going through all the heartache. There wasn't any way to separate my life from my art.

I had no idea if Damon and I had a future, but he'd changed me.

I stared down at the beginnings of the design and grinned.

Fucking beautiful.

Well, I guessed there was only one choice—I

had to invite him to the show. The big question was, would he attend?

✧ ✧ ✧

"GET IT TOGETHER, Sophia," I mutter to myself as I walk into the tower that houses Damon's office and his penthouse.

Maybe if I hadn't waited three full weeks since that night with Oliana and Karina at the club, I wouldn't have felt so nervous about extending an invitation to my upcoming fashion show. It wasn't like me to put things off.

Why was I being such a chickenshit?

Maybe it was the lack of sleep. Who was I kidding?

It felt surreal stepping into the lobby after all that had happened between us. I no longer lived with the enigmatic man who occupied the three-story ice palace that sat atop this building.

Calling it an ice palace was too harsh. Damon's home needed warmth and color to feel welcoming. The clean lines of his architectural project had pushed their way into the styling of his residence, giving it a cold, sterile feeling.

During the few short months I lived with him, I'd added small touches of my flair. It seemed to have softened the starkness of the giant penthouse.

I abruptly stopped as I approached the restricted access area of the building, pivoting to use the public elevators.

I no longer had the right to use Damon's private facilities.

Security knew who I was and probably wouldn't have said anything if I used it. But it felt wrong considering how I ended things with Damon the last time we were together.

My heart ached. For all that we were, all that we could have been, all that we lost.

I was here because of that night we spent together and the things Damon and I had done.

No matter how things were between us, I wanted him to know what we shared meant something to me. It literally inspired the centerpiece of my collection.

A slight pang of worry crept in as I made my way onto the lift and pressed the button for his floor.

Would I allow my feelings for him to overshadow everything wrong in our relationship?

He'd opened the doorway to my heart, and no matter how much I wanted to seal it closed, my love for him kept it open.

I blew out a deep breath.

Stop getting in your head and focus. Invite him to the show, leave, and no matter what, do not touch him. Your libido is not in charge of your body.

When the lift doors opened, I couldn't help but take in the incredible, unobstructed views of the city before me.

As an architect, Damon Pierce knew what he was doing. And with his office, he wanted to garner a reaction from when someone stepped on his floor.

I moved toward the floor-to-ceiling window, thinking back to all the times I'd taken the same view from the balcony a few stories above this very spot. I'd lived in a beautiful cage, but it was a cage. My freedom, life, and future were all on the line.

Nothing lingered over my head, but I still wasn't free.

Maybe once I launched my collection, I'd feel settled.

Taking the path around the elevators, I reached reception.

Ray, the front office clerk, recognized me and motioned with a hand to go through.

When I reached Damon's area of the building, I saw the walls making up his office weren't clear as he usually kept them during work hours, but they were tinted, and the lights were off.

That was odd. Was he out of the office today?

When I approached his assistants, Amanda and Taylor, I noticed they were preparing to leave for the day.

Taylor saw me approaching, and a slightly confused expression crossed his face. "Didn't Mr. Pierce contact you?"

"Why would he contact me?" I asked, stopping in front of him.

"To tell you about his grandfather."

His grandfather? All he'd ever spoken to me about was his siblings and mother. And also the fact he'd despised his father.

"What happened to him?"

"He passed away. A heart attack. I'm sure Mr. Pierce can give you the details."

I nodded, not knowing what else to do.

"When did he leave?"

"Yesterday."

"Thank you. I'll get in contact with him."

This made no sense. Damon had a living grandfather? Why hadn't he ever told me?

Was everything I knew about him a lie? Was the man I loved a figment of my imagination? Could I truly know a man who kept so much from me?

Without a second thought, I turned and went to Damon's private elevator, punched in the security code, then stepped inside.

As the lift ascended, I couldn't understand why he would keep this to himself.

When the doors opened into his entryway, my eyes caught on a pair of my discarded heels.

I'd left them there after an exhausting day of photo shoots. They were one of my favorite pairs of shoes. Still, after everything that happened, I decided only to have Lucian bring the essentials back to my apartment.

Why hadn't Damon put them away after all of this time?

Moving into the main living space, I found the rest of my knickknacks as I'd left them.

Nothing changed.

Well, except one thing. I walked over to the bar. There sat a giant basket of all of Damon's favorite sodas and a note from Lucian.

No more benders. You don't drink, remember?

Besides. Fuckers like you can't handle them.

Let me know when you're back in town.

-LM

PS: I took all your alcohol to keep tempta-

tion from getting the best of you. Also, fix this shit with my sister. Both of you are assholes.

I couldn't help but smirk at the last part of the message. Then, I focused on the bender and alcohol part.

He'd looked so unkempt when he showed up at the studio, and I never commented past saying something snarky.

My stomach dropped as realization hit me. "Oh, Damon. What have you been doing to yourself?"

He'd made a vow to never drink because of the abuse he and his family endured at the hands of his alcoholic father.

Why would he break it?

I shook my head, not understanding any of this.

"Idiot man, all he had to do was let me in, fucking talk to me. I would have been there for him no matter what he was dealing with."

Releasing a deep breath, I knew there was only one option for me to do. Damon shouldn't be alone, especially not at a time like this. I had to find him and help him, even if he didn't want me to be there for him.

CHAPTER NINE

Damon

"THE SUN SHINES on us today as we put Stuart Butler Pierce to rest."

Holding in a heavy sigh, I glanced up at the sky, hearing Father Connor's words.

I wasn't sure if the crystal clear weather was the Almighty's way of saying I was free of my past or a fuck you from my grandfather telling me he went out on his own terms.

Technically, he hadn't since he went out in an anticlimactic way. No fight, no rousing battle, only a heart attack due to cardiovascular disease.

It was the high-fat foods and candy bars that did him in.

For nearly a week, rain pelted the New England area. The hurricane the forecasters predicted to come in as a direct hit lowered to a tropical depression but soaked the area with torrential downpours, which left me putting this funeral off until today.

I scanned the area around me, completely unsurprised by the lack of attendees at the service. When a man who'd amassed billions through nefarious means and then fell from his high pedestal, no one wanted to associate with that man and risk soiling their name.

A small group of Grandmother Josephine's friends sat off to the side. They were here out of loyalty to her, not to pay respects to the asshole in the coffin. She probably wrangled promises out of them like she had done to me.

At least our oaths to the woman who deserved so much more than she'd gotten in life ended with this last act.

I narrowed my gaze as I recognized a reporter who'd written a piece about me for *Architectural Digest*.

The way he kept looking up and then down to type on his phone said he was either taking vigorous notes or composing some message.

Was he freelancing for some other news outlet?

Until Sophia entered my life, I'd enjoyed a quiet existence, keeping a relatively low profile with very little information about my personal life in public. Then, it all changed.

It started with jealousy getting the best of me

and pushing me to bring my relationship out into the open before Sophia's family and most of New York's elite. Then, it continued with the lengths I'd taken to protect Sophia during her battle to clear her name for Keith Randolph's murder investigation.

At this point, I gave a rat's ass about what he planned to do with the information he gathered regarding the funeral or my sordid family legacy of murder.

It wouldn't change the facts. Stuart Pierce was my grandfather. He died of a heart attack in prison after the State of New York convicted him for the brutal murder of his mistress and punished him with a life sentence with no possibility of parole.

If this snoop decided to write something about me and started a gossip frenzy, I would follow the same protocol I'd always followed—ignore every last motherfucker's questions until they got tired of asking them.

My annoyance with the reporter completely disappeared as I caught sight of a petite female sitting behind my grandmother's friends in the far back corner of all the seats. I wouldn't have noticed her if her demeanor wasn't so poised compared to the audience in attendance.

Why would any woman show up here? My grandfather hurt and abused women, destroying the essence of any female he encountered. The last thing he deserved was someone to show him any form of respect at his funeral.

In the next second, recognition filled me—the body, the regal jawline, the delicate hands. She wore all black with a large-brimmed hat and a lace veil meant to disguise her face, but nothing on earth could hide her from me.

Sophia.

She shouldn't be here. This cemetery wasn't the place for her. None of this evil needed to touch her. She was pure and deserved everything untouched by the taint of what I'd come from.

It was my fucking job to keep her safe and protect her, not bring her into the dirt and muck of my life, my lineage. All I'd ever brought her was danger and hurt her.

I only started to accept what we had was over and that staying away from her was best for us. She deserved so much better than anything I could offer her.

Now she'd shown up here, and the chaos churned inside me.

My logical and maybe cruel side wanted me to stalk over to her and demand she leave, tell her she wasn't welcome, that this was a private affair—the other part of me who couldn't imagine a life without her felt relief. I wanted nothing more than to take her in my arms and bury my face in her hair to inhale her comforting scent and have a few moments of solace from the shit that stewed around me.

Sophia cocked her head slightly, sensing my gaze, and lifted her veil to reveal her dark onyx eyes. My heart clenched, knowing she'd come for me.

After all the pain I caused her and the countless ways I disappointed her, she was near. The greedy or rather selfish part of me wanted her sitting next to me.

As if hearing my thoughts, she rose from her spot and gracefully moved toward me, taking the empty seat beside me. Without a word, she took hold of my hand and turned her attention to Father Conner.

✧ ✧ ✧

THIRTY MINUTES AFTER the funeral service ended, the last guest departed, and Sophia and I stood near the grave site. Neither of us spoke to each other. Our conversations remained limited to the guests and the priest.

It was as if we wanted to preserve the comfort of being together as partners to lean on without discussing the fact that we were in these roles.

Glancing down at Sophia's face, I noticed the dark smudges under her eyes and the sadness on her face.

"He isn't someone worth having compassion for. He wasn't a good man."

"I'm here for you, not him." She looked up at me. "You cared for him."

"I didn't," I replied so fast it almost felt like a reflex.

What would she think if I told her I despised the bastard, that I was happy to have the burden of his care lifted off my shoulders, or that I was ecstatic and relieved never to hear his fucking stories again?

"He meant something to you, even if you don't want to admit it. This funeral proves it."

She hadn't a clue.

"I'm fulfilling an obligation, nothing more."

Sophia took my hand in hers, turning to me. "Damon, this is me. I know what it's like to love people who choose to do horrible things my entire life."

"Your situation and mine are vastly different. I cared nothing for the murdering bastard. I made a promise to my grandmother. There is nothing more to it." I regretted my words the second I finished saying them.

But it was too late. I kept fucking up with her. She deserved so much better than the bullshit I brought to the table.

Her mouth tightened into a hard line, and a crease formed between her brow right before she said, "You don't get to shut me out like that."

"I'm sorry, Sophia. That was out of line." I shook my head. "This really isn't the place for you."

"Oh, you're going to tell me my place." The edge in her voice made it very clear she readied for this altercation. "Go ahead."

"You know that's not what I meant. I don't want this part of my life touching you."

"Why?"

"Because it's tainted."

"Get over yourself." She jabbed a finger into my chest. "I'm a Morelli, or did you forget this? The last thing anyone would think of us as was pure."

Grabbing her wrist, I flattened her palm against my suit jacket to keep her from poking me anymore.

I leaned down, bringing my face right near

hers. "Until I touched you, you were the definition of pure."

Out of nowhere, that familiar crackle of energy surged between us, and Sophia's pupils dilated.

My body responded to hers, craving her with the pent-up need for the weeks we'd been apart.

"I wasn't referring to that," she said with arousal lacing her words.

A light breeze picked up and snapped both of us out of the stupor we'd fallen into.

This wasn't the place for where our physical attraction was leading us.

Sophia closed her eyes for a brief moment as if to center herself and then released a deep breath.

"You're a good grandson. Just know our hearts give us the capacity to love or at least care for even the monsters of our worlds."

I opened my mouth to argue about my feelings for Stuart, but she covered my mouth with her hand.

"I should hate my father after the abuse of my childhood, the neglect of my teen years, and the pain he caused me after I left home. Hell, I should never want anything to do with him, knowing he was the reason for the mess of the arrest. But I love him. Flaws, broken pieces, horrible acts, and all."

"He doesn't deserve your love. Neither does your mother."

"I can say the same to you about your grandfather and father. But our hearts make their own decisions."

"I hate them."

She shook her head. "No. You hate that you loved them. No matter how horrible they were, it's natural for a child to care about the people in their lives. Even when we grow up, some part of us can't let go. You used the promise to your grandmother to keep ties to your grandfather."

I stared at her. A war of emotions churned inside me.

The urge to lash out at her and tell her to mind her own business sat on the tip of my tongue. I wanted to tell her to let me be and stop meddling in my life.

I couldn't do it.

Every word she'd spoken was the truth.

From the moment our eyes connected in Violent Delights, this woman saw to the core of me, pushing past my defenses and forcing me to face the truths of my life.

I wished I were more like my siblings. They'd washed their hands of anything to do with the Pierce family and bore no guilt for doing it.

Grandmother Josephine had asked them for the same promise of looking after and keeping in touch with Stuart. They'd agreed as a gesture to her, not because they had any intention to follow through.

Then again, Sean was the spare, and Claire was the girl. Neither of them had the pressure of being the heir to the empire. I'd lived under the thumb of the narcissistic asshole, father, and son duo, who drilled it into my head that I was responsible for their legacy.

"I have no idea why I kept returning to that damn jail every few weeks. Everyone we knew had washed their hands of him. All except my grandmother." I ran a frustrated hand through my hair. "He put her through hell. He used her wealth, abused her, cheated on her publicly, killed his mistress, went to jail, and she still forgave him."

Instead of saying anything, Sophia wrapped her arms around my waist, drawing me closer to her. Having her pressed against me calmed the rage brought on by the memories.

"He didn't deserve her," I said against the top of her head.

"But you did. Your grandmother stepped in when you lost your mother."

"She was more than a grandmother to Sean, Claire, and me. She'd not only raised us but took the blows meant for us. Alcoholics only wanted a target for their rage, so she made herself available to protect her young grandchildren. She should have been the one to live into her eighties, not this fucker."

"I wish I could say something to make it make sense, but I can't. I'm constantly questioning why things work out the way they do."

"You may not always tell me everything, but you never lie."

"There is only one thing I haven't told you, and it was because I made a promise long before I met you."

Yes, the reason why her alibi for the night of the designer Keith Randolph's murder had a huge hole. Whoever she protected had meant more to her than her freedom.

She slid her palm up between us to cup my face and then lifted a brow. "Annoying, isn't it when you're in the dark about the person you love?"

"Point well made, Ms. Morelli." I brushed my lips across her forehead and then rested my chin atop Sophia's head. "Is it wrong that I felt nothing but justice when I sold the company out from under Stuart while he rotted in jail?"

"No. If it helped you heal from your childhood, I say more power to you."

"I'm not sure it did. I used the excuse of the promise I made to my grandmother as the reason for ten years of prison visits, but maybe I put up with his crap hoping one day he would admit just once that he was wrong for what he'd done to Grandmother Josephine."

"I'm sorry. Men like that have too much pride to lower themselves to take accountability."

"What now?"

"You tell me. Why did you come here, Sophia?"

"To be here for you. Nothing more." She stepped back, holding my gaze. "You don't have to do everything alone."

"Then I take it that this isn't a reconciliation."

"No." She shook her head. "I stated my terms in my studio. We can't move forward until you accept them."

"You know all my secrets now."

"Not really. Perhaps in the future." She offered me her hand. "Come on. Let's get out of here."

"Where are you taking me?"

"Somewhere, so chaotic it will make it easy to forget about all of this for a little while."

CHAPTER TEN

Sophia

DAMON PEERED DOWN at me as if uncertain of what I planned for him. Our dynamic always had him in charge, knowing what to do and where to go. The control being in my hand more than likely set him off kilter.

Seeing his hesitation, I asked, "Do you have a wake planned?"

"Of course not. The last thing I want is gawkers standing around gossiping about the broken Pierce legacy."

"I thought you didn't care about what people said about you."

"I don't. My grandfather is gone, and it all ends with him. People say whatever the hell they want to say, but I don't want their vile words to catch up to my siblings. They have moved on."

Now, he could too.

No wonder he got along so well with Lucian. They were the eldest children of abusive tyrants.

Both tried to take the brunt of the attention whenever possible so the younger siblings wouldn't suffer.

"Then it's settled. You're joining me for dinner tonight." I moved past him, expecting him to follow me.

"I am?" He caught my upper arm, stopping me.

"Yes. You'll have rousing company and meet the rest of my clan."

A crease formed between his brows. "You're taking me to a family dinner?"

I nodded. No matter what Damon believed, he needed people around him, something to take his mind off his current situation.

Even if the Oliana and Karina invasion had annoyed me to no end at the time, it was the exact reset my mind craved.

Now, it was Damon's turn. Being with him showed me he rarely allowed anyone past his walls. Only two people ever managed it: Lucian and me. It's a good thing my plan involved both of us.

Suspicion lit his dark green irises. "Let me guess. It will be at your parent's house."

"Where else would we have family dinners? Most of my siblings are in town. This means my parental units will pretend to be on their best behavior. Which is always entertaining. You can even spend the night with me in my old room, and I can scandalize them with my sinful ways."

The energy immediately shifted between us, even though I hadn't meant to say the last part as it had come out.

My thoughts were to show him the room where I'd spent my teenage years and maybe have an honest conversation without the sexual trappings that seemed to get in the way whenever we were within the vicinity of the other.

Well, I screwed that up.

"I thought you said this isn't a reconciliation." Damon's fingers flexed against my skin.

Licking my parched lips, I watched his gaze flick to my mouth and then back to my eyes before I said in a much too husky voice, "I did, didn't I?"

"You confuse the hell out of me." He shook his head, released his grip on my arm, and threaded his fingers with mine.

I couldn't help but smile at that. "Welcome to my world, Mr. Pierce."

As we walked toward his car, he said, "Why do I get the feeling you planned to steamroll me into this from the beginning?"

"That's because you are very suspicious."

"It's because I'm right. Topping from the bottom, Sophia?"

I shrugged. "You allowed it, so I still won."

When we stopped in front of the passenger side of his car, instead of opening the door, he caged me with his arms and leaned down.

My breath grew unsteady, and arousal pooled between my legs. This was so fucked up. This man had me turned on in the middle of a cemetery following his grandfather's funeral.

"For this infraction, your Dom would punish you. Want to know what he'd do?"

I could only nod as my heart thundered in my chest, and the intensity of his presence rushed over me.

"After this dinner, he'll take you to that childhood bedroom, strip you naked, tan your beautiful ass red until you're begging to come. Then he will tie you to your bed, fuck you with his mouth and cock, making you come so many times that you can't think straight. However..." He paused, shifting his head to the other side of my face. "The punishment is that you'll have to stay quiet because your family is near and could hear what is happening. You don't want your brothers to know how you like it when your Dom spanks you, ties you up, or bites you. And you definitely don't want them to know you enjoy deep throating your Dom's cock so much that you have to slide your fingers between your legs to give yourself relief."

"What you are doing is cruel." I wasn't sure if my words begged him to go through with it or asked him to stop speaking.

"I'm not your Dom. You made that clear. It's only kinky sex. Isn't that what you said? I'm only telling you to imagine you with your Dom and a punishment of hot, dirty pleasure, all while you have to stay as quiet as possible."

He stepped back, immediately my legs wobbled, and I steadied myself by taking hold of his forearm.

He'd seduced me with words, with images of everything he'd done to me, could do to me. I ached for him, my skin burned, and I could barely breathe for wanting him.

That was when I heard his shallow exhalations. Lifting my gaze to his, molten lust stared at me.

"I got carried away."

"Most definitely." I dropped my head to his chest. "We need to go."

He cupped my neck under the hair at the

back of my neck. "We do."

"Sex isn't our problem."

"I know. The crux of everything is that you don't trust me."

"How can I trust you if I only know the parts you show me?"

"Today should show you I hide things for a reason."

"I want it all. I deserve it all. I won't let anyone make my choices for me again."

✧ ✧ ✧

AROUND SIX THIRTY in the evening, Damon and I arrived in Bishop's Landing. In less than fifteen minutes, we'd reach my parent's house right before the kids went to bed and smack dab in the epicenter of the chaos I'd promised Damon.

The Morelli family was what happened when all the predators in a zoo were released from their cages. Some part of me worried he would run the moment he experienced the crazy that was my family. The other part of me feared he would fit right in.

Either way, I'd find out soon enough.

At least, our ride here had settled into a familiar, comfortable space where neither of us needed to speak.

Only with him could I ever fill the time with nothingness. The arousal from before we left continued to hum between us, but it wasn't the essence of our time together.

I wouldn't lie to myself and say I didn't miss being with him like this, but I wanted more. I deserved more.

These weeks apart showed me we couldn't have a relationship unless he allowed me in.

"Who's going to be here tonight?" Damon asked as he neared my family property.

"Lucian and Elaine, Finn and Eva, Leo and Haley. And their kids, of course. Lizzy said something about trying to come home."

"Is she having problems at school?" The concern in his voice had me smiling.

Somehow, Lizzy was a soft spot for him. The baby of our family had a way of getting people to care about her. And since Damon had rescued Lizzy and me after our failed vigilante mob hit, it made sense that he'd want to protect her.

I shrugged. "No clue. She just said she needed a break. I don't question things. If you see her, you can ask."

"What about Daphne, Tiernan, and Carter?"

The mere fact he remembered them meant more to me than he realized. There were a lot of

Morelli siblings. Even more cousins. Most people lost count of everyone in the family.

Not Damon. He paid attention to everything.

If only he would just let me into his life.

"Daphne and Emerson are in Europe on an antiquities hunt. Tiernan is working on a charity project with Bianca, and Carter is somewhere tropical. I'm not sure exactly what he's doing." I thought for a second, trying to remember the last update Eva had given me. "Either he's on a mission trip or vacation. All I know is that he left with his partners almost immediately after Eva's wedding."

"I doubt many people have seen all of you in one place. I think the immediate family took up a quarter of the church."

"Well, not that much, but close." I pointed to a long drive leading to the rear of the estate. "Take that way. I hate going through the front of the house."

Once we parked, I guided Damon through the garden house and into the hallway near the children's playrooms. The sounds of my young nieces and nephews chattering and running around reached us the second we turned the corner. Added to it was the cry of a baby.

I started laughing, seeing the panicked expression on Damon's face. He looked ready to turn and run out the door.

It was time to remind him of his ulterior motives from a few weeks ago.

"This"—I pointed to my niece and nephew, who pretended to duel with foam swords—"is what happens when a sperm meets the egg."

The scowl he shot me had me laughing harder. "Why are you giving me a biology lesson?"

"Weren't you on a mission to impregnate me during that visit to my studio not long ago? I only wanted to remind you that if you were successful, this would result from the endeavor."

"I would have had nine months to get used to the idea." He gripped the back of his neck.

I patted his shoulder. "Keep telling yourself that. Come on. Let's go into the main part of the house. I probably should have brought you through the front entrance instead of the back. The kids' side of the house always scares the hell out of people."

"I'm not scared."

"Okay, I believe you." I rolled my eyes. "Lucian hates coming to this part of the house. He avoids it at all costs."

"But aren't half of them his?"

"Yep. He says his children turn into Satan's

henchmen when they are with their cousins." I tucked my arm into his.

"Let me guess. They're your henchmen."

"It depends on the day. Sometimes, they're mine. Other times, they belong to Lizzy. The kids love us since we aren't their parents and don't have to discipline them."

"Sophia Morelli, you're a menace."

"Still want to procreate with me? This could be your future."

He shot me a pointed glare. "My answer is going to stay yes. I want you. Having a child is the benefit."

"The night is still young. You haven't sat with Bryant and Sarah Morelli at a dinner table."

"I won't change my mind."

"That's good to know. Although we both know this isn't about changing your mind but mine."

"You will."

"Don't get ahead of yourself. I make no promises."

"Eventually. Even if it takes years, you will."

"You have the stamina to wait that long?"

"You're well aware of my stamina."

"What makes you so sure? Don't forget, I have stipulations."

"I could never forget. And to answer your question. There is one very good reason you will change your mind about us."

"That is?"

"You love me," he stated.

Before I could reply, Lucian said, "That's interesting. Since she hasn't mentioned you in weeks. By my book, you no longer exist in her world."

"This is between Sophia and me, Morelli. Get lost."

"Not happening. She is my baby sister. What I say goes when it comes to her."

"Oh, the hell you do." My temper flared, and I stalked over to my busybody older brother and poked him in the chest. "Did I, or did I not, tell you to stay out of my personal life?"

"You said something I chose to ignore."

"Damon is your best friend. Why are you so against us?" I glared at Lucian, so ready to clock him in the nose. Knowing him, he'd probably laugh if I tried.

"I'm not. Pierce doesn't get to tell you what to do."

"But you do? I will figure this out on my own. I don't need you to come to the rescue."

Lucian glowered down at me. "If you kept me

in the loop, you wouldn't have ended up in half the shit you found yourself in over the years."

"They were my mistakes to make. How many times do we need to go over this before I hit you with a chair to get it into your head?"

"I'm your big brother. I have a right to be involved in your life."

"I'm not twelve. Get over yourself. Where's Elaine? She'll take my side." Then I shouted, "Elaine, I need you to get your husband before I kill him."

A hand crept around my waist, and the next thing I knew, I was behind Damon, with him holding me tight against his back.

"Let's take it down a notch." The amusement in Damon's question added to my annoyance. "I have to give it to you. Your family is a hell of a lot more interesting than mine ever was."

"I'm glad I can entertain you."

"Is this what you meant by inviting me to dinner to take my mind off things?"

"Not really, but I'm improvising. Want to let me loose so I can use Lucian as my test dummy?"

Damon's arm tightened around me. "Not a chance, killer. You're staying right behind me until you calm down."

"For fuck's sake, Pierce. You don't need to

protect me from her. What the hell is she going to do to me, scratch me with her nails?"

"Let me show him what I can do with these nails." I clenched my jaw and pushed Damon, hoping to get around him so I could punch my smart-ass brother. Or maybe I'd just pretending to do it because it's taking Damon's mind off the funeral. "Oliana taught me more than enough moves to fuck him up."

Damon kept a vise grip on my waist, refusing to budge no matter how much I thrashed.

"What is going on in here?" Leo rushed in, followed by Elaine, Leo's wife Haley, Lizzy, and Eva.

They all came to a halt and took in the sight before them.

"I'm so confused," Lizzy said, breaking the silence. "Who's fighting who?"

"Our idiot brother and me." And since this whole thing proved we were all still two-year-olds, I decided to add, "He started it. Lucian doesn't know when to butt out."

Lucian looked up at the ceiling as if he were praying. "Someone deliver me from this insanity."

"You started it. Now you have to wallow in it." I smirked at him.

A throat cleared, and then Eva gestured with

her chin. "I hope you realize the children watched this whole interaction."

In unison, we all turned our attention to the hallway leading to the playrooms.

Five children of various ages stood in the archway, each with interest and fascination on their little faces.

Of course, Lizzy had to get the littles involved in this mess. "Kiddos, did you see what happened?"

They all nodded.

"Then you know who started the argument?"

They nodded again.

"Who's the guilty party?"

They pointed to Lucian in unison and said, "He is."

"I told you they were Satan's henchmen," Lucian muttered and then stalked out of the room.

✧ ✧ ✧

"You're a pain in the ass, you know this?" Lucian said as he refilled my wine.

"It takes one to know one." I lifted my glass, and he followed the gesture before we both sipped.

"The two of you make no sense. One minute,

you're ready to slaughter him, and the next, everything is sunshine and roses." Damon's look of confusion had me laughing.

"You'll get used to our crazy," I assured him.

"I highly doubt it."

Lucian leaned forward. "Sophia and I are the black sheep of the family. We have to stick together. Because of that, she can't stay mad at me for too long. Isn't that right?"

"More like you'd keep showing up everywhere I went until I gave in." I rolled my eyes.

"Same thing."

Leo, Eva, and Lizzy looked up from their spots around the large dining room table with smiles.

"This is how we are," Eva spoke. "We fight, we yell, and then we get over it. Occasionally, it takes a little time and convincing, but we stick together."

A knowing glance passed between Eva and Leo. They'd always shared a special bond, just as Lucian and I had our way about us.

"Morellis hate passionately." Dad decided to join in on the conversation now that he'd downed his third glass of wine. "But we know when to put aside our differences."

Hopefully, if he was mellow, he would keep

with the relaxed atmosphere for the evening.

"I only wish all of my children understood the meaning of loyalty and family." He stared between Lucian and Leo.

And my hopes were dashed.

"We're here, old man. Get over yourself," Leo muttered.

"Ungrateful. All of you." Dad picked up his glass, downing the rest of the contents. "The only good thing that's come from you especially are my grandchildren."

Damon leaned closer to me and whispered, "Is this his version of good behavior?"

"As close as we will get," I answered and then added. "I promised you a distraction. Am I delivering?"

"Most definitely. You Morellis always deliver on your promises."

CHAPTER ELEVEN

Damon

"YOU SHOULD HAVE let him win," Sophia said as she led me up the stairs to her childhood bedroom. "He's a terrible loser."

I remembered earlier in the evening when I'd beat Bryant in a chess match. He hadn't seemed too put off by losing from how he'd continued with the conversations and other games. Yes, he'd grumbled about missed opportunities, but nothing others would have said in the same situation.

"He seemed to have taken it well enough."

She shot me a sideways roll of her eyes, and continued forward. "Believe me when I say Dad will hound you for a rematch. He thinks he's the ultimate chess player and won't stop until he wins against you."

"He's good but no match for me. Even Lucian has only won a quarter of the games against me, and he's ten times better than your father."

"Jesus. Keep your voice down." She covered my mouth. "The last thing I want is for Dad to hear you say that."

I moved her palm from my lips, unable to hide my smile. "Are you worried your father will hate me and I won't get his seal of approval?"

I gave him an undignified snort. "No one has a say about the man in my life but me."

"Then why the worry?"

"Comparing Lucian and Dad is the ultimate sin in this house. Their relationship is volatile on the best of days."

"That's because your father created a more ruthless and better version of himself in Lucian, hoping he could control him, and it backfired."

She held my gaze as if reading something in my soul. "Is that what happened with you and your father and grandfather?"

I swallowed, not even realizing how my statement about Lucian paralleled my upbringing until Sophia pointed it out.

"You're very insightful, Sophia Morelli."

"I only call them as I see them. Come on." She gestured with her chin. "Let's not loiter. I want to change into something more comfortable."

A few minutes later, she opened the door to

her room. At first, I could only stand in the entryway and take in the space.

Modern elegance was the perfect way to describe it. Neutral shades of textured wallpaper covered the walls, and strategically placed silver and gold accented fixtures gave the room a glamorous feel. The gemstone chandelier added a touch of regalness, and the four-poster bed with its plush covering announced only someone with class slept there.

"This isn't you," I said before thinking twice about it.

"How do you know?"

"Because I've been around you. I lived with you. This is a bedroom for a magazine, not for the Sophia Morelli I know."

I slowly scanned the space and walked inside. There was no feeling of the warmth I felt in Sophia's studio or her apartment here. The thought of her growing up in this type of environment infuriated me.

With so much love and compassion inside her, this woman deserved a family who showered that upon her.

"Is there any part of this room that you see is me?"

I slowly found genuine pieces displaying Sophia's passions, dreams, and joys. She placed everything in a fashion so as not to intrude on the display of perfection for the public.

"That tucked-away shelf holding your sewing supplies. The basket with the fashion and design magazines next to the bed on the side with the windows. The sketchbooks you have stacked between all the classic novels on the bookcase. And the dress form sitting inside the left corner of your closet."

"It isn't fair that you see all of me, but I'm only allowed glimpses of you." The rawness in her words tore at me.

"I'm working on it."

"We'll see."

I moved toward her but stopped when she headed into her closet. She'd changed into a sleep set when she stepped out, making me narrow my gaze.

"We sleep naked, Sophia."

"In this house, we don't. Besides, we aren't together. You're lucky that I will let you share the bed with me. I could be mean and tell you to sleep on the floor."

"Always the brat."

✧ ✧ ✧

"No, no, no. I don't want to hear anymore. Please, no more."

I jolted up hearing Sophia's panicky cry. I blinked rapidly, trying to clear the haze of sleep, only to see the darkness engulfing the room all around me.

"Why wouldn't he leave me alone?" Sophia's anguish tore at me.

I turned on the light and found her curled in the fetal position, covered in sweat and shivering. Pulling her to me, I lifted her into my arms and held her close.

"Sophia, wake up. You're safe. No one will hurt you. You're safe."

She shook her head. "He's always around. I punched him. Now he wants to make me pay."

My stomach dropped. Sophia was reliving the time after that fucker Keith Randolph assaulted her.

If he weren't dead already, I'd take great pleasure in killing him slowly.

The only solace in this was that his father's empire sat on the cusp of falling. Randolph Senior had catered and covered up his boy's deeds and now sat poised to defend himself on a slew of charges from bribery to murder.

I pushed the damp hair off Sophia's face and

repeated, "You're safe. I won't let anyone hurt you."

Sophia opened her eyes with another whimper and stared at me, not saying anything.

After a few moments, she jerked, trying to sit up, but I held her close. "Damon. It's you."

"It's me."

She dropped her head against my shoulder and wrapped her arms around me as if trying to hold onto a lifeline.

"Make me forget these nightmares. I don't want to remember the past."

I inhaled deeply, knowing what she asked of me. "Sophia, you don't want this. You'll regret it in the morning."

"You don't get to tell me what I want or what I'll regret. No one will make my decisions for me ever again." The edge in her voice had me looking down at her.

Tears soaked her cheeks. However, the determination in her eyes made it impossible for me to deny her anything.

I shifted us, laying her onto her back, and leaned over her.

God, she was breathtaking.

The contrast of her fire and vulnerability pulled at something deep inside me. I wanted to own, consume, and revel in every part of her.

Brushing my lips over hers, I teased her with soft, gentle passes, wanting to drive up her desire and eliminate any remnants of her nightmare.

Her fingers threaded into my hair, and she pulled me closer, desperate to deepen the kiss. In response, I nipped her lower lip, causing her to whimper, and took hold of her wrist, pinning them to the mattress above her head.

"You wanted me to make you forget. That means I'm in charge."

"You're always in charge."

"I'm the Dom. You hand me your power, and in exchange, I give you pleasure."

I expected her to deny my role as her Dom, to fight me on my claim.

Instead, she said, "I want all the pleasure you can give me, Damon. I'm desperate for it."

A knot in my stomach I hadn't known existed unfurled.

Her stubborn nature may want to deny what we were to each other, but she knew the truth deep down.

I trailed my tongue down the shell of her ear and along the column of her neck. Goose bumps prickled over her skin, and she grabbed hold of my shoulders, digging her nails in as she arched up and lifted her pelvis to rub her pussy against my straining cock.

Out of instinct, I pushed into her, loving the feel of her heated cunt. After all of these weeks, burying myself in her balls deep would be a pleasure unlike any other. However, it wasn't possible here.

"I won't fuck you in this house. I value my life too much."

Her heated gaze connected with mine, amusement touching her swollen lips. "But anywhere else, you would?"

"Absolutely."

"As long as your nefarious plans don't include impregnating me, I may accommodate you."

I couldn't help but shake my head and chuckle. "You never say anything I expect."

"Isn't that part of my appeal? I'm unpredictable."

I stared down at her, unable to hide the emotions welling up. "Your appeal, Sophia, is that you make me feel."

"Then let me in."

"I'm trying."

She pursed her lips. "Hmm."

Instead of using this time to argue my point, I kissed her again. She met my demands. Our tongues dueled, tasted, savored.

I tugged down the minuscule tank she wore, revealing her perfect breast. Enclosing a nipple, I laved it until it was hard and straining.

She bit her lower lip to hold back a moan as I moved to the other sensitive bud, giving it the same treatment.

Her legs wrapped around my thighs, gyrating harder along me to gain the friction she needed. My cock wept, wanting to meet her siren's call and fuck both of us into oblivion.

But this wasn't about me. Sophia's pleasure was all that mattered.

I worked free of the grip she had on my hips and slid down her body, letting my mouth and hands create a path of sensation from the valley of her breast, along her toned belly, to the waistband of her sleep shorts.

Her breath grew unsteady, and she clutched at the sheets beside her. I took hold of the elastic band of her shorts and drew it down her thighs and knees. However, I left them around her calves to restrain her and pushed her legs wide open for me.

She glistened with her arousal, like an offering for me to feast upon.

"You have the most beautiful cunt, Sophia. I

love how you're always so wet and ready for me." I blew on her exposed pussy.

She squirmed and then brought a fist to her mouth, trying to stifle a moan.

"That's right. You have to keep those sexy sounds quiet. You don't want your family to know how you begged me to pleasure you."

I took a swipe through her slit, lapping up her delicious essence. I fucking loved the taste of her.

She gasped, and her back bowed.

"I—I don't beg."

I flicked and circled her clit with my tongue. "Just like you aren't submissive. Am I correct?"

"Shut up and make me come," she ordered.

"Tsk, tsk, brat. For that, I'm going to make you wait." I pushed two fingers inside her pussy, pumping in and out as my mouth worried her sensitive nub.

"Please, Damon. Don't do that to me. I need to come. I'm desperate."

"That's how I like you. Panting, aching, unable to think of anything but me."

I gorged on her. I held her right on that precipice of release, her inner walls quivering and flexing but unable to reach that point needed to contract completely.

Her hips pushed off the bed, and a sheen of

sweat covered her skin.

"Oh, God. Let me have some relief. I haven't come in so long."

"How long?" I asked. "A day, a week? Do your toys not give you what I can?"

"Why does it matter? I'm desperate. Damon, please." She grabbed a pillow and covered her face as if to stifle the symphony of her pleasure.

I had to hear more. I cupped Sophia's ass, pulling her entirely against my mouth, and lost myself in her taste. My tongue licked, flicked, and devoured her dripping pussy while my hand worked her core, pistoning a steady rhythm.

When I knew she was mindless with the need for release, I asked, "What did you use the last time you came, Sophia? Your hand, a toy? Tell me."

She writhed and arched, tossing the pillow to the side and shooting me a murderous glare. "Your cock."

"My cock?" My lips curved. "I guess I did ruin you for anything but me."

"You conceited asshole."

Instead of responding to her insult, I bit down on her clit and, at the same time, stroked the sensitive bundle of nerves deep inside her pussy. Her orgasm erupted, her muscles clamped down on my fingers, and her arousal flooded my mouth.

She rocked against me, and she pressed her lips together in a desperate attempt to keep her cries from escaping. She began to lose the battle as her release continued to ride through her.

I slid up her body and covered her mouth, taking in her moans of pleasure. Watching her fall apart was an experience I'd never grow tired of seeing.

When her body relaxed and her breath eased back to a manageable level, she said, "What have you done to me that I only want you?"

"I'm your Dom, Sophia. You might as well accept it. Your orgasms belong to me. Your submission belongs to me. You'll only ever desire my eyes anywhere on you, my touch on your skin, and my taste on your lips."

"No."

"Yes."

"This is only kin—" I covered her lips with my palm, cutting her words off.

"This is more, and you know it. One day, you'll forgive me."

She pulled my hand away. "I've already forgiven you."

"But," I added, knowing it would come.

"I'm not sure I can trust you to give me all of

you. I shouldn't have to stumble across your past. You have to be open with me."

"What can I do to get you to trust me?"

"You can start by telling me the whole story about your family. And…" she hummed. "Also, add in another orgasm or two."

I smiled, dropping my forehead to hers. "In that order, or can I mix it up?"

"You decide."

"Good answer."

"See, I'm not always a brat."

CHAPTER TWELVE

Sophia

A LITTLE BEFORE eight, I entered the house through the back entrance, following a five-mile run around the family property. Damon left for his place an hour earlier, needing to grab a change of clothes and freshen up before starting his workday.

I still reeled from how he consumed my senses last night. I'd asked him to make me forget, and he'd delivered. My skin continued to burn with need from the way his hands and mouth seemed to have worshiped every part of me.

The only thing that would have made it perfect was if his cock joined the fun.

But then, the whole house would have heard us since it had taken all of my strength not to scream at the top of my lungs from the delicious torture Damon had put me through with his wicked tongue.

It also blew me away that he explained the

details of his family history. His past was as sordid and full of scandal as the Morellis, sans the dozens and dozens of legitimate and illegitimate children.

My heart ached for the boy he'd been and the pain he'd suffered under his father's and grandfather's thumbs. It explained the bond Lucian and Damon shared.

Like were drawn to like, they both were the eldest sons of abusive fathers who only thought of themselves and their legacy.

Damon opening that door into his life gave me hope for us, but something still held me back.

Maybe I still harbored some anger about what happened between us at the club. When I told him that I'd forgiven him, I meant it.

I knew why he'd done it. He wanted to protect me. As stupid as he was for making my choice for me, he wanted the best for me.

See, Mom, I could be an adult about situations.

I sighed and accepted the truth. It all stemmed from what I'd grown up around.

What if I risked it all with Damon and ended up in a situation like my parents?

I couldn't do it. I just couldn't.

No matter how much I loved Damon. I needed more in life than financial stability and status in society. I wanted companionship, friendship, joy, laughter, respect, and, most of all, deep love. My parents had none of this. They were attracted to each other, but the violence and the forced sexual acts between them in no way represented a healthy relationship.

They were the poster couple for never getting married.

Pushing off my sneakers, I set them on the shoe rack, slid on a pair of house slippers, and strode toward the kitchen.

Time for a large cup of coffee.

I'd barely taken five steps when Lizzy came barreling toward me.

"Sophia, where have you been? I was looking for you."

I frowned. "I went for a run after Damon left. What's going on?"

"I need to talk to you." She tugged at my arm, dragging me toward the empty playroom.

Digging my feet in, I jerk us to a stop. "If you want this conversation to remain private, I suggest a different space. Don't forget about the baby monitors."

"Shit. You're right." She grabbed my wrist and pulled me into a receiving room no one used, but Mom had decorated and ready, just in case the occasion arose.

Once inside, she closed the door and locked it.

"What's going on? And why did you come home this weekend?" I cocked a hand on my hip, waiting for the answers to my questions.

"I have to ask for a favor."

"Not until you tell me why you're home. The last time we had a real conversation, you told me you had plans for the next three weekends. What changed?"

Lizzy dropped her head, turned away from me, and sat on the chaise near the window. "I need to get away from some people."

The protective side of me flared to life.

"Who?" I asked, sitting beside her and taking her hand in mine. "Are you in trouble?"

If Lizzy got into a situation like mine, I wanted her to know she had someone in her corner. I'd never turn my back on her.

"No, I'm fine. I'm not used to living with people who aren't family."

I studied her, not believing a word she said. "Is it a boy?"

Her head snapped up, a glimmer of shock in her dark eyes.

Bingo.

"It has nothing to do with a boy." The resignation in her face told me she was lying through her teeth.

I knew that look. I'd seen it in the mirror plenty of times since Damon and I separated.

Continuing to press, I asked, "Then is it a man?"

"Sophia," She huffed. "All that matters is that I'm home for the weekend and need a favor. Are you going to help me or not?"

"It all depends on what you want me to do?"

"Hey, you owe me after our adventures in vandalism."

I cringed, remembering how Lizzy and I dressed as prostitutes, broke into Keith Randolph's Penthouse, and destroyed his spring collection. We'd barely made it out of the place without getting caught and, in the end, had to call Damon to rescue us and give us a ride home.

"Fine. What do you want? But if it's dangerous, I'm not doing it. My guilty conscience is still paying penance for letting you tag along in my vigilante mission."

"Will you take me to Violent Delights?"

I coughed, never in my wildest dreams expecting to hear my innocent sister ask me for a favor like that.

"Absolutely not."

Lizzy jerked her hand free of my hold, a crease forming between her brows. "How is it fine for you to be there and not me? I'm a legal adult. I have a right to visit a kink club."

She had me there.

"Why do you want to go?"

"Because I want to understand the draw of BDSM. The internet and books only give so much information."

"You researched it?"

"Yes." Her annoyed glare reminded me of something I would have given Eva.

"Sorry, I just wanted clarification."

"Then let me make something else clear. I know you're into kink."

I rolled my eyes. "Duh. You asked me to take you to Lucian's club."

"How about this? I know you met Damon there."

I lifted a brow. "Outside of Eva and Lucian, no one knows this. How did you find out?"

"I'm not twelve. I see things. I listen. Everyone in our family has secrets and preferences they think I don't know about."

"And you want to go to Violent Delights to explore your preferences? Is that what I'm hearing?"

She nodded. "I'm curious. There are things about me I want to understand. I looked up clubs near campus but decided against going there."

I sighed in relief. "Don't step foot in any of those places, Lizzy. Most of those clubs aren't safe."

"I know this. That's why I'm asking you to take me. I really don't want to have to talk to Lucian about this."

I gaped at her. "You were going to talk to Lucian if I said no?"

"Please, Sophia, don't make me do it. He's an asshole on the best of days. I don't need his million and one questions."

The fact she even contemplated going to Lucian meant she was seriously interested in exploring how she felt about kink.

I would have loved to have someone I felt comfortable with to take me into Violent Delights the first time I stepped inside the heady energy of the club. I'd been so excited and overwhelmed. Having someone with me would have eased my anxiety.

"Okay. But it will have to wait until next week sometime. I need to put the finishing touches on the showstopper."

"It's about time. You've worked on it nonstop

for the last few weeks. I guess that means I'm coming in for fittings soon."

"I have a few last touches to add, and then I'll call you in."

"So, back to my request. Do we have a deal?"

I sighed. "Yes. Once I feel I'm at a finishing point, I'll take a break, and we can visit the club."

Lizzy wrapped me in a tight hug. "Thank you. Now I can relax. Oh, by the way, Mom's on the terrace outside the kitchen. She said something about wanting to talk to you. You might want to go in there. She's probably annoyed since our talk took longer than I expected."

"Thanks a lot for the advanced warning."

Lizzy gave me a sheepish smile. "You're welcome."

Just as I left the room, she added, "Oh, by the way, she's in a weird mood."

"What do you mean?"

"I don't know how to explain it. Something seems different about her. It's not our normal mom. Like she's fragile, maybe she's getting sick. Who knows?"

"Okay, I'll go see what's up."

✧ ✧ ✧

"You wanted to chat with me," I said to Mom

as I strode onto the terrace with a cup of coffee and a warm blueberry muffin.

Mom set her mug on the table before her and glanced in my direction. "Come sit."

Taking the seat across from her, I settled in and waited for the conversation to start.

I took in her appearance, noting Lizzy's observations were spot on. Mom's demeanor today was different as if she'd forgotten to slip on the mask she wore daily as her shield.

Her energy almost felt approachable and open, which, for some reason, frightened the fuck out of me.

The woman before me wasn't the mother I knew or understood.

She remained quiet for a few more heartbeats as if gathering her thoughts before she said, "I always wondered what kind of man you'd bring home. Damon Pierce wasn't anything in the vicinity of what I imagined."

"What did you expect?"

"Someone more," she paused, her lips curving at the corners. "Eccentric."

I lifted a brow. "Eccentric?"

"You must admit, the people in your circle have interesting reputations."

"True." I grinned back at her. "You do know,

Damon isn't normal by any means? And I'm positive the rumors about him have reached your ears."

She nodded. "I've heard things."

"Doesn't it bother you?"

"I'm more interested in whether or not it bothers you."

"It doesn't."

"Then I don't care either."

Who was this woman, and where had the aliens put my mother? Why was she being pleasant?

This couldn't be real. Damon must have burned all my brain cells away with his orgasms.

"Do you plan to marry him?"

No was on the tip of my tongue.

Instead of saying that, I responded with, "I can't answer that unless he asks."

"And if he asks?"

I looked away, took a steadying breath, and then decided to give her the truth. "I don't know. I never planned to marry anyone. I promised myself never to fall into a marriage like the one you have with Dad."

Shit. Maybe I shouldn't have been so blunt.

Instead of annoyance or hurt on her face, she nodded as if accepting what I had to say.

"Do you hate me, Sophia?"

Without hesitation, I answered, "No, Mom. But I don't understand you."

"What is it you don't understand? I'll answer any question you have."

I sat there, not sure if this was a trick. Then, I glanced around, noticing we were the only ones on the terrace outside of Mom's personal security team.

Well, she opened the door. I was going to step through it.

"Why did you put up with all of the things you did? Why did you let him use you and do those things to you?"

Mom shook her head as if to deny what I was saying, and I lifted my hand to keep her quiet. Nope, she wanted to go here. We were going.

"I know what I heard and saw from my room next to the library. It wasn't my imagination. I didn't make it up. All of it happened."

Her face lost its color, and she swallowed a few times. "I'm so sorry you had to see and hear any of it. I should have moved you long before you could understand it."

Yeah, instead, there was a production of it being my birthday gift to move to a grown-up room, and when I refused, she made me out to be the ungrateful daughter.

Oh, fun times.

"That's not my point, Mom. Until today, you didn't even acknowledge the things I heard or saw actually happened."

"It isn't something a mother wants to admit to her child, Sophia."

I took a deep breath, knowing a level head was the only way to discuss this. "I remember how thin the walls between my room and the library were and the countless times Dad ordered you onto your knees so you could suck a man's cock. I can remember times when you cried and begged him not to make you do something, and then later, you were screaming and moaning. I was too little to understand what was happening in the beginning."

Mom looked away from me, her cheeks flushing with embarrassment.

"Then came the day it all cleared up. You know the day I'm talking about, don't you, Mom? The reason you moved me into my big girl room."

A tear slipped down Mom's cheek, and she nodded.

"I'd come home from school because I was sick, and no one knew except the household staff.

I saw Dad and another man fucking you while you lay on the pool table in the library."

"You shouldn't have been there. You should have stayed in your room." She covered her face with her hands.

"And continued to listen to you crying and begging him not to make you do it? When everything grew silent, I thought he either killed you or dragged you away, so I went to see. I was a child who didn't know better. These are my first experiences with sex."

"I agreed to it. Bryant didn't force me into it."

"I was there, Mom. Who are you trying to convince? You or me? You fell in line with everything. You accepted the abuse. Why? It makes no sense."

"What do you want me to say? My relationship with Bryant isn't a storybook tale, but we understand each other. It's how we remained strong for nearly forty years."

"Can you at least admit to me that your marriage is toxic?"

She lifted a glass of water, drank the liquid, and nodded. "Fine. I admit it. It still doesn't change the fact our marriage works for us. We have something greater than love. We're bound by loyalty."

I stared at her as if she'd lost her mind. My parents cheated on each other constantly. Hell, they had children with other people. What the fuck kind of loyalty was that?

"I don't understand this loyalty you're talking about."

Mom gestured around her. "Bryant and I created this. The Morelli legacy and everything that comes under its umbrella, the money, power, status, this mansion, and so much more. For everything we did and all that I endured and sacrificed, I reap the rewards now."

"What kind of marriage was that? You essentially sold your soul for material things. Are you honestly happy?"

She gave me a weary smile. "That's all relative. When I married, I didn't have much choice in the matter. It was a business deal between my father and Bryant. Within two years of saying my vows, I learned to accept my new world's rules or let them run me over."

"You were barely a mother to us."

"I can't change my behavior. To survive, I became the wife Bryant wanted me to become."

I stared at Mom, seeing how vulnerable she seemed right now. Tears soaked her cheeks, and without her makeup, she wasn't Sarah Morelli, the matriarch of the Morelli dynasty, but a woman molded into something she probably didn't even like herself.

No matter how much I wanted to rage at her for hurting me throughout the years, I couldn't do it. For the first time in my life, she was honest with me. She bared her soul to me.

She was a victim, just like those women in the shelter where I volunteered. So many of them told stories of the things they'd done that they wished they hadn't. They'd lied, they'd hurt others, they'd stolen, but it was the only way to survive, to protect themselves and the ones they loved from mental and physical abuse.

At this moment, I truly understood the saying, you can love someone and hate them as a person. The statement summed up my feelings toward Dad.

"The reason I never wanted to marry was because of the way Dad treats you. He controls you with money, status, this life." I rubbed my temples. "I refuse to marry unless it's something deeper."

"Who said you can't have that?"

I lifted my head to look into her deep blue eyes. "How is that even possible for me when all I know is this?"

"If it's happened for your brothers and sisters, why can't it for you?"

Her words had me pausing.

I thought back to last night and how everyone interacted. Until Elaine, no one would have believed Lucian had a beating heart. The laughter and joy they shared spoke of a deeper connection. It was the same for Eva with Finn and Leo with Haley. They balanced the other. There was never a competition for who ruled. Each couple wanted the best for the other.

A tinge of sadness hit me. Could I risk trusting Damon again?

"Sophia, answer this question for me. Do you see a happy life without Damon?"

Logically, I knew I would survive without him. I had survived without him and thrived.

But had I been happy?

I shook my head. "No."

"Then don't limit yourself because of the mistakes I made."

"Can I ask you why you decided to have this talk with me?"

"You really want to know?"

I rolled my eyes. "Yes."

"You're not going to like hearing this, but you are the most like me of all my children."

I frowned, and Mom laughed.

"It's true. I was like you when I was young. I made your grandfather crazy with my antics. I want you to keep that spark."

"That still doesn't explain why you decided on this conversation."

"I saw the way you were with Damon. He's reserved but has no problems with you being you. You spent the evening saying outrageous things, and he wasn't embarrassed or irritated by you or your actions. In fact, he seemed to find your antics amusing. And then, by the end of the evening, your easy way with everything had him relaxed enough to challenge your father to a chess match and not let him win, knowing how he pouts."

"I still don't get it."

Mom joined her hands and lifted them with her head up to the sky. "Mother Mary, give me peace."

"What did I do wrong?"

"Sophia, I don't want you to lose the joy like I did. If you pick someone like your father, you will. With someone like Damon, you won't."

My throat burned as I put the pieces of everything Mom said together.

"What if it doesn't work out?"

"You have choices. You'll figure it out. You always have."

I nodded, "Okay."

We sat in silence for a few minutes. The weight of resentment slowly lifted from my shoulders.

"Well then. Now that we've finished with the heavy stuff. I want to hear about your collection. I'm sure it will scandalize me."

I stared at Mom, unsure if I would burst into tears or start laughing. This was the mother I longed for, the woman I never ever expected to exist under the skin of the person I knew all of my life. How had I gotten here with her?

It made no sense.

But I refused to forsake my blessings. I planned to hold on to this moment for as long as I could. I knew Mom would have her mask and armor on soon enough. At least for now, I had the mother I dreamed about as a child. The mom who wanted to know about me and understood me, even if it was just for a short breakfast.

CHAPTER THIRTEEN

Damon

I GRIPPED THE back of my neck, ready to throw the blueprints rolled out in front on the drafting table in front of me across the room. No matter how hard I tried, I couldn't concentrate on the changes a client requested for a new project.

I wasted another day because I couldn't keep my head in the game.

It only took one night with Sophia for her to consume every one of my thoughts again. Even before she'd shown up at the funeral, she constantly lingered in the back of my mind. I couldn't stop wondering where she was and what she was doing.

Nothing had changed in our relationship. We'd given each other comfort, nothing more.

I had to keep reminding myself of this, or I'd never get my head on straight.

Then why the fuck did it feel as if everything had changed? At least for me, it had.

Outside of my siblings, she knew more about me and my fucked-up family history than anyone else.

After over a decade of friendship, Lucian only had bits and pieces I kept hidden away from the public.

I knew nothing I shared with Sophia would ever leave her lips.

I trusted her in a way I had never trusted anyone in my life.

From the beginning of our relationship, I told Sophia everything with us was her choice, and then my actions contradicted my words. No wonder she continued to keep that wall up between us.

The prime example was how I acted that night in her studio. I hadn't even worked to get her back, and I expected her to move back in with me and make plans for our future.

The number of times Sophia told me I was arrogant was too many to count. I'd taken it as our form of banter and her being a brat, but she'd done nothing but speak the truth.

I was arrogant and focused on what I saw as the right way. This left her afraid.

I was supposed to be her safe place, her security.

I sure fucked that up.

Letting her in and baring my soul to her was the first step to fixing the mess.

Now what?

In the three days since I left the Morelli estate, Sophia and I hadn't seen or spoken to each other.

I wanted to give her space and resisted going to her studio.

But what if I'd read the situation wrong? Was she waiting for me to make contact?

At this point, I had no damn idea what to do. I was a grown fucking man, wandering around like an idiot.

Pushing back from my chair, I approached the floor-to-ceiling windows in my office and gazed out at the Manhattan skyline.

After heating the streets throughout the day, the sun filled the sky with a perfect late-afternoon glow. It invited the people of the city to come out and enjoy the approaching evening.

In contrast, everything inside me felt cold, lonely, and isolated. It wasn't something I experienced until I lost Sophia.

I craved Sophia's fire. She represented warmth and vitality. That was why all her things remained as she left them in the penthouse a few floors above me.

I needed to see them and remember how she'd brought life into my world.

I'd closed myself off for so long and now paid the price.

My phone buzzed on my desk with a series of texts. I glanced at my watch, seeing it was close to six o'clock. The messages were probably from the different crew leads sending me updates on the various projects around the city.

This meant I was now officially off the clock. Not like I was doing any damn work anyway, but whatever.

Releasing a deep breath, I scanned the skyline one last time and decided an ass-kicking in the gym was what I needed to help me get my head on straight.

An hour and a half later, I arrived in my penthouse, sore and feeling somewhat better after a hard workout.

Throwing my things on the kitchen island, I moved to the fridge when my cell flashed with more incoming texts.

What the fuck? Silencing the thing made no difference if the strobe light would blind me.

I grabbed the mobile and read the display, seeing Lucian's name on the screen with an indicator saying there were five messages from him.

Whatever the asshole wanted me to do for him tonight. The answer was, a big fat get the hell out of here, no.

I couldn't care less what incentive he dangled in front of me. I had no energy for a clean-up situation, and the only Morelli I wanted to deal with anytime soon was currently out of reach.

When my phone rang with an incoming call, I groaned. Then, seeing Lucian's number flash on the screen shifted my annoyance to concern.

If he called, that meant it was urgent. What the hell had he gotten himself into?

I answered, "What's wrong?"

"Is that how you answer a phone?"

"It is when you blow up my phone with texts and then call me before I get a chance to read them."

"What the fuck was the point of me texting you two hours ago if you don't read the messages?"

Two hours ago? Fuck. He was the one messaging me in the office.

"Some of us work, Morelli. What do you want?"

"Scan the messages and tell me what you're planning so I'm prepared. I was giving you a heads-up earlier. Now things are different."

I frowned, putting him on speaker. "Could you get any more dramatic? Hold on, let me look at the messages."

When I pulled up the text, my blood ran cold, and I asked Lucian, "Who's the friend?"

I scanned the messages, wanting to kill whoever this fucker was with my bare hands.

> **5:46 Lucian:** Do you know where my sister is going tonight?
>
> **5:46 Lucian:** She made a reservation for two. Who the fuck is she bringing with her?
>
> **5:47 Lucian:** Did I or did I not revoke your membership, asshole?
>
> **5:52 Lucian:** She's coming with a friend. Do you know this friend? When the fuck did this happen? I thought you two fixed things.

Lucian's response made me want to eliminate him, too. "Does it matter? All Ventana told me was that Sophia arranged a guest pass with him for a friend. He's having cocktails with her now. Violent Delights."

I clenched my jaw. "Sophia is already at Violent Delights?"

"She arrived fifteen minutes ago."

"Who is her guest?"

"That isn't your issue."

The hell it wasn't.

"Are you going to let her participate?"

"She's an adult. She can do whatever she wants."

"She's mine. No one touches her but me."

"You don't get to make that call, Pierce. She does."

"What aren't you telling me?"

"If you want her, I suggest you find a way into the club."

"Did you forget you revoked my membership?"

"When has rules of any kind stopped you from doing what you wanted?"

"I know what you're doing. You're looking for some excuse to shoot me."

"I don't need an excuse. What I want is for my sister to be happy. Figure it out, jackass."

Lucian hung up.

I stared out from my kitchen into the expanse of my living room. A well of possessive agitation churned inside me. Why would Sophia go to Violent Delights without me?

Had she decided to move on? Was she looking to replace me?

I'd assumed we'd crossed some barriers the other night.

Dammit. What was happening right now? I had to get it together.

No, this wasn't Sophia. Something was driving this.

I would find out what it was.

She was fucking mine. Mine.

✧ ✧ ✧

I PULLED INTO the parking lot of Violent Delights, taking a spot near the entrance of the brownstone building. Stepping out, I tossed my keys to one of the attendants. She knew who I was and wouldn't say anything to me. As far as most people were aware, I was still a member.

What I needed to worry about was the security wall I'd have to pass through to enter Violent Delights. And this barrier was guarded by the managing partner and gatekeeper, Clark Ventana. Lucian may own the place, but nothing happened inside the club without Clark knowing.

We'd been friends at one point, but now that remained to be seen. The incident with Sophia caused a strain between us that seemed to grow wider by the day. I wouldn't deny that I deserved it.

I'd broken the club's rules under Ventana's watch and ignored Sophia's safeword. Even if I staged the situation to fit a plan, I'd broken my oath as an original club member.

As if waiting for me, I'd barely taken two steps toward the glass doors of the lobby when they opened. In front of me, Clark leaned against a counter with his arms crossed and a scowl on his face. Positioned behind him was a wall of security guards who somehow managed to seamlessly coordinate their uniform colors with the mahogany walls of the club.

Clark's frown grew into a sneer as he stood, and his tailored suit gave him more the aura of a hit man than the head of a kink club.

I strode toward him, ready for this confrontation.

"Where the fuck do you think you're going?" Clark asked, standing to his full six-foot-two height.

If he intended to intimidate me with this stance, then he'd failed miserably. We were about the same size in build and height. And we'd mastered hiding the danger we posed to people under our expensive suits.

I knew he packed some muscle since we'd worked on a few clean-up situations together. However, in this situation, if he blocked me in any way, I would run his ass over to get to Sophia.

"I'm here for Sophia."

"Interesting. After your performance with her the last time you were here, I wouldn't have expected the two of you to continue your arrangement."

"What's between us is none of your business, Ventana. Now get out of my way."

"No. She has a right to be here, and you don't." Two bouncers flanked Clark. "I revoked your membership."

"Morelli reinstated my membership when he informed me Sophia was here."

He lifted a brow as it was news to him. "Until he passes this information on to me directly, you aren't going anywhere."

"I will see her. She is mine." The thought of anyone touching her sent a wave of anger boiling up inside me.

I tried to push past Clark, but his wall of muscle grabbed my arms and held me in place. There wasn't any use in trying to fight them. These assholes were twice my size and would have me pinned to the ground in seconds.

"She's not a possession, Pierce." Clark got in my face. "You don't own her. She makes the call on who she is with, not you."

I was starting to hate this fucker. From the

beginning, Clark explicitly made it clear I wasn't good enough for Sophia. He'd introduced Sophia to every other Dom in the club except me.

"Who did she bring here?"

"It's not you. That is all you need to know."

"I'm not leaving without her."

"You will when I throw you out on your ass."

"Let's not be too hasty, Mr. Ventana," I heard an amused voice behind me. "Mr. Pierce wants to see me. Well, here I am."

Immediately, my attention shifted to Sophia. The curve at the corner of her lips told me she found the scene before her entertaining. However, the energy and intensity I saw when I gazed into her dark eyes felt like she waited and expected me to come.

"He's not a member. And therefore, not permitted on the premises."

Sophia shot him a sideways glare. "How often did I sneak in here before becoming a member? Let him pass. I'll vet for Mr. Pierce."

"You're the one he broke the club rules with, remember?"

"You know he staged it. You heard the playback and saw parts of the video—time to get off your high horse." She pursed her lips.

Oh, Sophia. Always the brat, even with the

head Dom of Violent Delights.

No matter where she was, Sophia had no problems telling someone where to shove it. Clark Ventana was the reigning king when Lucian wasn't around, and she couldn't give a shit.

Clark stepped in front of me to block my view of Sophia. "You can do better than him."

"I'm not interested in any of your other candidates. Accept it."

I clenched my fists, ready to pull free of the gladiators holding me hostage and punch Clark in the face.

Clark sighed. "If I allow Pierce in, you're responsible for him. That means your membership is on the line."

"When did you become so dramatic, Master Ventana?"

"Remember where you are, Sophia. And who I am." Clark's warning pushed all my buttons.

If he laid one finger on her, he was a dead man. "You fucking touch her, and I will kill you, Ventana."

"It's a matter of respect, Pierce."

Ignoring the outburst, Sophia skirted around Clark to face me. She pushed the hands of the security off my shoulders and arms and took my hand in hers.

Then she looked at Clark and said, "It was never my intent to show you any disrespect. However, I believe there is something about me you haven't realized in all the times we've interacted."

"What is that?" Clark watched me with suspicion.

"Since I entered this club, I have always been me. Always Sophia Morelli, always Lucian Morelli's little sister, always the possible submissive looking to explore. I never pretended to be anyone but me at all times. And I always know you are the head Dom of this club and my brother's friend."

"Where are you going with this?"

"I flirt and joke with you while keeping that in the back of my mind at all times. There is no separating the two. I accept who you are. I respect you, but I won't let you treat me like a child because you see me as a little sister."

"Are you saying I treat you differently based on the situation?"

"You wouldn't have asked that question if you didn't already know the answer." She focused on me, and the intensity of so many things unsaid between us pulsed as if they were living things. "If you'll excuse me, Master Clark. It is time for me to escort Mr. Pierce into the club."

CHAPTER FOURTEEN

Sophia

Holding Damon's mesmerizing emerald gaze, I offered him my hand.

Without a word, he slid his palm over mine, and I drew him toward me, ignoring Clark and his security team.

A shiver slid down my spine, and goose bumps prickled my skin as my nerves fired to life. This man's mere presence affected me in ways I couldn't explain to anyone.

I guided him through the front hallway and toward the lounge.

"How did you know I was here?" I asked, wondering who could have called him.

"Lucian. He called me."

"Really?"

He was the last person I expected to contact him, considering his behavior toward Damon over the last few months. Would I ever understand their love-hate relationship?

Damon nodded. "Now, I'll ask you the same question."

"The bartender, Tate, saw you pull in during his break and came to inform me that you arrived."

It was more that he'd rushed in since he'd heard the rumors about Damon's revoked membership and decided I needed to head off a physical altercation.

In addition to making some of the best drinks I'd ever tasted, Tate kept his eyes and ears on the pulse of gossip in and out of the club. And since he liked me, he never wanted me blindsided by a situation.

"In other words, he wanted you to play interference between Ventana and me."

"Something like that," I smirked.

He paused, turning toward me and gripping my waist, his intense gaze making my heartbeat accelerate.

A crease formed between his brows, and his fingers flexed where he held me. "Did you come here to find another Dom?"

What would he say if I told him that I wouldn't have come if it wasn't for Lizzy?

From the moment I stepped through the doors earlier in the evening, memories of Damon haunted me everywhere I turned—of the things we'd done, of the intensity of the first time we met, our many scenes together, even how he'd broken my heart.

And because Lizzy knew nothing of my history in the club, I kept quiet, resisted the urge to run from this place, and put away the discomfort of being here without Damon.

Lizzy wanted to explore her craving for kink, and I couldn't deny her this request, especially when I had access to a safe and comfortable space like Violent Delights.

"No," I shook my head. "If you recall, the Doms of this club did nothing for me. That's why you found me sitting at the bar the night we met."

"Then who is your guest? Are you planning to scene with them here?" He clenched his jaw, making it dawn on me that he believed I brought another man here with me.

"I can't believe you're jealous," I stated with a grin. "Why would I jump from your bed to someone else's in less than a week?"

"I'm not jealous. I'm possessive. You knew this when I claimed you. Now answer the question."

"Oh, okay, Mr. Pierce." I shook my head while I laughed and slid my arms up his chest.

"Fine, if you really want to know who I brought with me, I'll tell you."

He fisted my hair, tugging my head back. The bite of it sent a shiver down my spine and arousal pooling between my legs.

"I'm waiting."

I licked my lips. "I came with Lizzy."

"Lizzy? Why would you bring her here?" The confusion etched over his features was almost comical.

I lifted a brow. "The same reason I came here. To explore."

"I see."

"Do you?"

He shook his head. "No, honestly. I haven't a clue what is going on between us."

My heart clenched. For a man so sure of himself, I'd turned his world upside down.

"Remember when you promised to ruin me and make it so no other man would ever live up to you?"

"Yes."

"Well, you accomplished your goal. You ruined me, Mr. Pierce. I only want you ever to touch me."

"Do you understand what you're saying, Sophia?"

I swallowed, thought of my conversation with Mom, and then said, "It is you who has to accept things. I was all in, and I thought you were too. Then you changed your mind, and you pulled back."

"I never changed my mind about you." Just as I was about to respond, he cut me off and continued, "But I hear you. There is no pulling back anymore or in any way. It's my vow to you."

My lips trembled for a second as I took in his words.

Nodding, I said, "Good. I need to get back to Lizzy. I'm sure she's talked Tate's ear off by now."

"She's not old enough to drink. Why is she at the bar?"

"I had to leave her somewhere when I learned a certain Dom decided to storm the castle."

He frowned. "You're having too much fun at my expense with this."

"I am, aren't I," I grinned, pivoting in his arms and threading my fingers with his.

We entered the lounge and immediately noticed the attention of many patrons shift in our direction.

Ignoring their stares, we made our way to the bar. Lizzy's eyes widened when she caught sight of Damon and me.

Tate said something to Lizzy, pulling her attention back to him and making her laugh before they began some back and forth banter.

"He does his job well," Damon observed.

"That's why it was easy to hide out with him when I couldn't find anyone interesting."

"Looks as if Lizzy will take your place at the counter since someone has now piqued our interest."

"Is that an order or a statement?"

"It's a fact."

"Really? Who established this?"

"Your Dom." My core spasmed, hearing those two words delivered in that deep, commanding tone of his.

Desire and need hummed inside me, waiting, churning.

"I have a Dom? That's interesting. Since when?"

He gripped my hips, stopping me from going any further. "From the moment my cock took that cherry of yours. No, before that. It was when I watched you walk into this room the night we met."

"If I recall, I told you that I wasn't a submissive."

"Yes, I remember. You were exploring. However, with me, you play one role and one role only." His breath coasted over my ear, and my skin heated as arousal pooled between my folds, and the throbbing deep in my core grew to an ache.

There was no point in denying the truth. "Only with you."

"Only with me," he agreed.

Lizzy rose from her seat and moved in our direction. There was no hiding my flushed face or the fact something more than a conversation had occurred between Damon and me.

As she neared, she gave me a once over and cocked her head to the side. "Everything okay?"

"Nothing to worry about. Do you want to continue the tour?"

"Yes, but not with you." She gave me a smirk and glanced over to Tate.

"Why? What's wrong with me?"

"Nothing is wrong with you. I don't need you for this."

That's when it hit me. Lizzy wanted to do this without me. Well, not really me, but not me, as in her sister.

I nodded. "I get it. You're an adult and don't need me looking over your shoulder."

"Exactly. Besides, who's going to eat me in

Lucian's club?" She rolled her eyes. "Everyone knows who I am. They are all scared for their lives."

I had to give it to her. Her annoyance was valid.

"Just so you know, I had Clark as my guide here, so don't believe I was ever completely alone."

"Then find me someone other than you to follow me around."

Damon stepped between us. "I have the perfect person for you. Give me one moment."

He gestured to someone, and a few seconds later, Foster, a club member who was also a submissive, approached.

The awe on his face at having Damon call him over had me remembering Damon's reputation as one of the most coveted Doms in the club.

His skill was legendary, and for him to ask a submissive to participate in a scene was considered an honor.

And then I came along and messed up the way of things.

"Lizzy, this is Foster. He is a house submissive. Foster, this is Lizzy." Damon gestured to Lizzy's blue wristband, signifying she was completely new to the kink world and not available for play. "She's interested in seeing demonstrations and learning more about the lifestyle. Keep her safe for me. No one is to speak to her without permission, and she is not available to anyone for a scene."

"Nothing will happen to her. I promise." Foster's enthusiasm reminded me of an adorable puppy who wanted to please.

"Lizzy, you good with this?" I had to ask her.

Instead of giving me a straight answer, she tucked her arm into Foster's and waved goodbye.

From the shell-shocked expression on Foster's face, he was probably reconsidering his agreement to Damon's request.

"What happened to Lizzy in college over the last few months?" Damon asked, seeming confused by Lizzy's behavior. "She is a completely different person now than the girl I met after your vigilante incident."

When he said the last part, he shot me a smirk, which had me pursing my lips. Yep, that night wasn't one of my finer moments.

"She's trying to figure out who she is. Just like all of us do."

"Have you figured out who you are, Sophia?"

I turned to face him. "Some. I'm a work in

progress."

"As I've discovered recently. We all are." Suddenly, something wicked entered his eyes, and he offered me his hand. "May I have the privilege of your company this evening?"

A shiver slid down my spine. Damon said those exact words to me in this very spot the night we met. That was how I'd fallen down the rabbit hole of Damon Pierce.

I'd intended it to be one night to lose myself in the world of kink and then return to my mundane life.

Then he'd shattered my plans, and I'd never been the same again.

I smiled at him and gave him the same line I'd spoken many months ago. "You wouldn't have come over here if you didn't believe I'd say yes."

"A real gentleman always asks." His eyes sparkled with humor.

I slid my palm over his. "We know you are no gentleman when it comes to sex, Mr. Pierce. You're positively unhinged."

His pupils dilated, and my core spasmed.

"That's not the line." He curled his fingers around mine and drew me to him, bringing his face a few inches from mine. "Did you forget our initial conversation?"

"No, I remember every word." I gazed into his heated emerald depths. "But, I know you better now. My revisions are much more accurate."

"And what is the verdict on this side of my personality?"

I licked my lips, and his focus shifted to my mouth for a fraction of a second before returning to my eyes. "I prefer this to the façade of the gentleman."

"Are you saying I wear a mask to hide my true nature?"

"Don't we all? Some of us are better at disguise than others." I rose onto tiptoes to rub my cheek against the stubble along his jaw. "Though, I prefer it when you don't wear anything."

"Is that a hint you want me naked?"

"I—I'm not hinting," I said through a shallow breath. "I'm making it very obvious. You denied me the other night. I want restitution."

"We were in your parent's house."

"Are we there now? You need to service me, Mr. Pierce."

"Service you? I believe you misunderstand the dynamics of this relationship."

"My comprehension is very sound. Are we—" I hesitated and glanced away, afraid to ask the question on the tip of my tongue.

"Are we what?" He tilted my chin up. "In a relationship?"

I nodded.

I hated feeling so vulnerable. I was the one who pushed Damon away. I was the one who kept resisting, and now I felt like an unsure teenager who couldn't understand any of her decisions.

"Yes, irrevocably."

"Do you even know what that last word means?"

A crease formed between his brows, making me smirk. "That mouth of yours will get you in trouble one day, brat."

"Let me know when the day comes."

He coasted his lips over mine. This gentle teasing was as seductive as his fingers stroking other parts of my body.

A moan bubbled up from my throat, and I leaned forward, desperate to taste him.

However, he caught me by the throat, his palm a heated brand, sending a shiver down my spine.

I lost myself in his hypnotizing green eyes, and my breath grew unsteady.

"The day is today. Let's go."

CHAPTER FIFTEEN
Sophia

I BARELY HEARD Damon's words, so lost in the press of Damon's fingers on my skin and the surge of arousal cascading throughout my body.

Since that night in the public playroom, when he'd pushed me to my knees, we kept all of our scenes private. At this moment, with the desire coursing through me, I'd let him bind me and fuck me for all to see.

I licked my lips and asked, "How do you plan to punish me, Master Damon?"

"You'll find out soon enough." He shook his head. "And since when did you start calling me Master Damon?"

I shrugged. "I have to change it up occasionally to keep things interesting."

"Always the brat."

"You know you love it."

"True."

My heart skipped a beat, hearing his response.

"Damon," I whispered, unable to hide my emotions.

His lips curved at the corners as he released his hold on me and then trailed his fingertips along my jugular, between my cleavage, and around my waist to my lower back.

"Come with me, Ms. Morelli."

As if in a trance, I moved with him down the path leading to the private playrooms for the elite members.

He sealed us inside with a click of a lock and walked me to the middle of the room. All I could do was stare into his intoxicating emerald eyes and bask in the whirlwind of emotion he rarely revealed to anyone. Well, anyone but me, it seemed.

My throat burned, and my heart pounded as if ready to explode.

What was this man doing to me?

He leaned forward, kissing me, seducing me, intoxicating me. I wanted more. Oh, so much more. My nipples beaded and strained as my breasts swelled, begging for attention.

Pulling back, I nipped his bottom lip and watched his pupils dilate, turning his eyes into dark green rings. In the next second, something wicked entered those emerald depths, and I gasped and arched against his hand as it slid along my bare labia.

Wait. When had Damon undressed me?

I glanced down to see I only wore the corset that cinched my waist and exposed every other part of me.

How had he removed the clothing under it without me noticing?

Those damn eyes of his had hypnotized me, that's what it was.

Amusement touched Damon's lips as the haze he'd cast over me cleared.

Evil, evil man.

That's when I took in the room around me. It was so different from all the ones we'd used before. Hedonistic was the only way to describe it. Rich colors of reds, greens, and blues decorated the space, with pillows, sofas, and lounging furniture strategically placed everywhere.

"Are you ready to play, Sophia?" So much desire laced his question, sending a shiver down my spine.

"Yes," I said, and then, without thinking, I dropped to my knees and placed my fingers on the button of his pants.

He fisted my hair, holding me in place. "Did I tell you to do that?"

"I'm improving on your plan." I stroked his erection through the material, feeling him grow harder and longer.

"You do this. There will be consequences afterward." The sinful intent in his words had heat blooming deep into my pussy.

"Is that a promise?"

"You'll beg me to stop. You'll even consider using your safeword."

I narrowed my eyes at him and continued on my mission, lowering his zipper and freeing his beautiful, engorged cock.

Fisting him from root to tip, I said, "You don't scare me, Damon Pierce. You won't win this time."

"This isn't about me winning, Sophia." He jerked me forward until his bulbous crown grazed my mouth, coating my lips with his precum. "It's about your submission—to pain, to pleasure, to what only I can give you. I will take you to the edge of what you can take and bring you back."

Was he planning the same thing he'd done the night he shattered my heart? Anxiety settled in the back of my mind.

"Is this a test for you or me?"

"You'll have to wait and see." He pushed past my lips, keeping me from responding and forcing me to take him back.

He groaned his pleasure, the sound so arousing, so exciting. My breast ached, and my clit throbbed.

Jerking my head back, he set the tip of his dick on my lips right before he shoved in, hitting the back of my throat and holding himself deep.

I forced myself not to gag, to remember how to relax my muscles. Tears spilled from my eyes.

This was so brutal, and for some insane reason, I fucking loved it.

I pressed my thighs together, my core quivering and clenching, so desperate for something to fill it.

He moved my head back and forth, not giving me any control of the pace. I worked him up and down with my hand and my mouth, letting the tip of my tongue lave the pulsing vein along the base of his cock.

All the while, I held his lust-filled gaze.

The man had this savage beauty about him that drew me. Because of him, I had a new collection. He'd inspired so much of it.

His breathing grew more unsteady, and his hold on my hair tightened to the verge of being too painful.

His cock swelled in my mouth, and he

clenched his eyes and jaw tight before he gritted out. "Take every damn drop. Don't let anything spill out. I want you to suck me dry."

I barely readied when he held me against him, shuttering and coming in hot, hard spurts. The salty, sweet essence filled my mouth, and I could only swallow.

I ached everywhere, needing relief. Damon pulled me off him. Immediately, my strength faltered, and my face dropped to his thigh as I gasped and trembled.

After a few seconds, he tugged me to my feet and held me against him.

Once our breaths calmed, he glided his palms up the side of my body.

I lifted my gaze to see the unleashed desire still coursing over his features. However, a predatory light had entered his green irises.

As if sensing my thoughts, his lips curved slightly, and he said, "Turn around."

Without hesitation, I followed his direction and stopped in shock as I faced a Saint Andrew's Cross.

Had that been there this whole time?

How had I missed it?

I really needed to pay attention to my surroundings.

I studied the beautiful piece of equipment and all of its intricate details.

It wasn't like the ones in the other rooms. It seemed to be made of a higher quality wood as if it were a custom piece with thick padding and soft buttery leather overlay.

At the four points where a person's arms and legs would attach were lined cuffs made of the same high-quality material. Then, there was the magnificent design work etched into the wood. Only a master craftsperson could have achieved that level of artistry.

No way was this some ordinary Dom's playroom.

"Who does this room belong to?" I asked, hearing the rustling of clothes.

His warm fingers settled on my hips. "No one. It's open to the top Doms in the club."

"Meaning it was Lucian's until he stopped coming here."

He used his body to walk me forward, pressing my torso to the bisecting beams. "It is ours for tonight."

Pushing the thought of my brother to the back of my mind, I focused on Damon. He'd completely stripped while I studied the Saint Andrew's Cross. The heat of his chest on my back was a heady contrast to the cool, soft leather material against my front.

The way his arms reached around me, caging me, made me feel safe, cocooned.

He took hold of a cuff and attached my wrist to the top of one side of the cross. Then, I repeated the process with my other hand. He stretched me out, exposing me back to whatever he planned.

My skin burned and prickled with goose bumps. The throbbing deep in my core intensified as my desire coated the inside of my thighs.

I knew what he was doing. Going slow to heighten the expectation, the need.

He surprised me when he fitted my ankles to the bottom of the equipment, positioning me in the complete shape of the Saint Andrew's Cross. This wasn't something I'd experienced with him before.

I wouldn't have any control.

How could he know I craved this desperately? To not think, to lose myself in the experience, to hand myself over. With him, I was safe. With him, there was pleasure. With him, I could let go.

His shallow breathing told me he was as affected by this as I was.

He came up behind me, his thick, hard cock a

brand along my back. I squirm, rubbing his length, which only heightened my arousal.

He slid his fingers between my pussy lips, finding my clit and stroking.

"You are so wet, so ready."

I couldn't help but whimper, "I ache."

"Do you?" He pushed two fingers inside me as he continued to tease the sensitive bundle of nerves. "Let me give you a small bit of relief."

He drove deeper into me and then curled his digits, finding that spot that felt oh-so-good.

I bucked, unable to help myself, letting my body lose itself in the pleasure he brought over me. Then, in the next second, my muscles tensed, and I shattered as exhilaration and pure, unadulterated ecstasy filled my body.

He pulled out of my spasming pussy, letting me ride out my orgasm. Slowly, his palms slid up my sides, and he cupped my breasts, pinching the tips with an almost too-painful grip.

Throwing my head back, I clenched my eyes tight.

I loved it. I wanted more. And right before I begged Damon to keep going, he pulled away.

What was he doing? This couldn't be it.

I'd barely finished the thought when searing agony scored across my buttcheeks.

"Oh God," I cried out, my breath caught in my throat.

Was that a whip, a crop? I fucking had no idea.

"Breathe, Sophia. Breathe."

Gasping in large gulps of air, I followed Damon's directions.

Oxygen filled my lungs, and the pain morphed into delicious, heated pleasure.

The following strikes came in succession, sending me into a headspace where it sat in the back of my mind that I wanted none of the pain. Still, at the same time, I needed more, and I'd demand more if he dared to stop.

My pussy quivered, never truly coming down from the earlier release. It built upon the endorphins pumping in my system, and now my body seemed too tight.

What had he done to me?

I wanted Damon in me, my pussy, my ass, my mouth. It didn't matter where, as long as I had his cock.

"I need you. Please."

"Oh, you don't get me until you come at least four more times."

"Are you crazy? That is completely impossible."

"Challenge accepted."

"I didn't say—"

He smacked my swollen pussy with his open hand.

I detonated, throwing back my head, and called out, "Damon."

My core contracted and released, so desperate for something to fill it. The pleasure of it wasn't enough. This wasn't enough.

Tears poured from the corners of my eyes. I teetered between heaven and hell, unable to decide if oblivion awaited me or an endless precipice.

"I love it when you cry, Sophia," Damon murmured as he tugged my head back by my hair and licked the wetness along my cheeks. "You are so fucking beautiful. And all mine."

"I hate you."

He chuckled. His green eyes were a mix of lust and mischief.

"Do you?"

Evil bastard.

"No."

"That's what I thought. Three more to go, then you get my cock."

I sobbed, "You're going to kill me."

"I'm loving you. Nothing more."

"Asshole."

"There she is. I was wondering when the brat would appear." He covered my lips, seducing me with his taste.

I loved how he engulfed my senses as if he were a storm cascading over me.

He broke the kiss with a curse, "Fuck. It's so easy to lose myself in you."

His unsteady breath and the flush on his face should have given me satisfaction, but it only heightened the pulsating desire rolling around inside me.

Knowing I had the power to affect him in this way comforted me as well as intoxicated me.

"We begin again." He took hold of the crop, bringing me to the cusp of orgasm.

However, this time, he kept me on edge, ready to tumble, wanting nothing more than to unknot the coil holding tight in my core.

"Damon, what are you doing to me?" I panted in unsteady breaths.

"You'll figure it out soon enough." His hands gripped my thighs, wedging his shoulder in a way I was spread open for him.

His tongue speared my pussy, pushing in deep.

My body reacted, flying over the cliff he'd

pushed me toward with the crop. He kept thrusting in and out, eating at me. Then he fluttered over my clit, lashing it with wicked strokes.

I whimpered and bucked, unable to come down from the high.

He sucked my sensitive bundle of nerves, drawing on it, laving it.

Out of nowhere, I climaxed again. My pussy quivered and wept all over Damon's feasting mouth.

When he moved away, all I could do was sag in my restraints. My body was no longer mine.

"Ready to call it quits."

"Never. You promised me your cock."

"I did." A humming sound reached my ears.

In the next second, something cool and wet touched me. I thrashed and jerked against my bonds. I couldn't think. I wasn't sure what I felt.

It was too much—too much stimulation.

I was dying. I was sure of it.

Then he pushed a slick object into my pussy, the vibration a torment meant to destroy me. He worked it in, stretching my walls. The girth of the dildo felt so much broader than Damon's cock. It was almost too much to handle. Then, with some harness, he fastened it to my waist.

Oh my God, he was going to leave it in me while he administered more of his pleasure torture.

"One more to go."

Maybe I couldn't take another one, no matter how much I wanted him to fuck me.

"No more, please, no more." I could barely focus on anything but the sensations in my pussy.

"You know how to stop this."

"Will you listen if I do?" I taunted him, unable to hide my agitation.

"You already know the answer to that." He pressed his finger along my too swollen and hyper-sensitive clit, circling round and round. "Would you like to continue with the crop or move to the cat or the whip?"

"What?" I tried desperately to clear my head and focus on his question, not the pulsing between my legs.

Crop, cat, or whip. Crop, cat, or whip.

When the crop landed, the heightened pain level numbed my mind and sent me on a ride of euphoria.

The cat-o'-nine-tails gave a bite meant to sting and singe the skin, then leave a dull ache I craved more.

The whip wrapped itself around the body in a

wicked caress and then disappeared, leaving its mark of breath-stealing, searing agony and delicious bliss.

I closed my eyes, taking in shallow breaths. My brain wasn't functioning. He couldn't seriously expect me to decide.

Then, before I realized what came out of my mouth, I answered, "Whip."

"This won't take long, and then I'm taking that beautiful ass of yours."

"You can't be serious."

With the dildo and him inside me, filling me so tight, I wouldn't be able to take even the slightest inhale.

"Your cunt is occupied."

The first crack of the whip hit the air. It wasn't until a second or so later that I felt the warm sting across my bottom. The icy, hot pain followed, and soon afterward, a dull, delicious ache replaced it.

"More," I gasped. "Do more."

"Greedy," he teased.

"Yes. You knew this."

Another strike landed across my back.

"Fuck," I gasped.

This one burned. The pleasure wasn't as fast, coming slower, in a tingle.

Three came in succession, my mind whirling with the onslaught of pain and elation.

Dizziness engulfed me.

Another series scored my calves, my thighs, my ass.

I arched with the little movement I could manage into each kiss of the whip.

What was he doing to me? I wanted more of this insanity. I had to come. I needed to come.

My core spasmed and flooded around the dildo.

The stimulation confused my body. The sensations were too much for me to orgasm.

"Damon, please. I can't come without you."

He stepped up behind me, pressing his hot, naked form to my tender back. His cock wedged itself along my labia, hard, thick, a brand, ready to push into me.

I couldn't help but love the feel of this and revel in the bliss of it.

I felt what he had planned. I knew the bite of it would be well worth it.

I wanted to tell him to hurry, but he'd only make me wait.

He kissed my shoulder and asked, "Is this what you need?" Right as he smacked my aching pussy with an open hand.

I threw my head back as my release washed over me. It was agony and gratification rolled into one. A lubricated finger pressed into my ass. I clenched around it, feeling how the movements in and out of me spurred on my ride.

"Breathe through this," Damon instructed, his arm snaking around my waist.

My thoughts were unable to comprehend what he meant until realization hit me.

He replaced his finger with the large bulbous head of his cock.

"Are you out of your mind?"

"Do you want to use your safeword, Sophia? Have I taken you too far?"

My mind whirled, my skin burned, my body ached.

Damon was cruel, evil, demented.

Was this his new way to push me, to see if I'd break?

Fuck him. He should know by now I wouldn't do it. Not this time.

He wouldn't win.

"I won't say it. You can't make me. You're not getting out of this ever again."

"You still believe I want out?" He pushed past the ring of nerves in my ass, making me grit my teeth at the pleasure-filled pain, and, at the same time, he increased the speed of the vibrator in my pussy.

I jolted as an onslaught of sensation poured through me. "It's too much."

"Oh, Sophia. Tell the truth, is it truly too much?" he rocked his hips, tunneling deeper and deeper.

I couldn't breathe. I couldn't think.

With me in this position and the large dildo filling me, there was no way he could fit all of himself inside me. He'd tear me in half or kill me.

Beads of sweat slid down my face, and my core quivered.

If I actually died this way, would it truly be such a bad way to go?

"Tsk, tsk. Ignoring me will only get me to push you further." He pulled out and slammed in, seating himself balls deep.

I screamed.

Was this bliss or agony? Right now, I couldn't tell.

I wanted to cry out my safeword, tell him to stop, and at the same time, beg him to move, ask him to push me further, and take me to the finish line.

There was no sense to any of my thoughts.

He held still as his lips grazed my neck and

then the shell of my ear. "Now tell me, is it too much? Are you ready to stop? Do you want to say your safeword? Or."

His palm shifted from around my waist, over my bare stomach, and between my folds to where the vibrating toy continued its unrelenting torture.

I knew his fingers rested on top of the controls. He wanted to see how far I'd let him take me.

This time, he used pleasure or the promise of it as the means to take me to the point where I'd use my safeword.

"Or?" I pressed.

"Do you want me to continue pushing you, teasing you, making you question your sanity and all that we have before I send you over that cliff where bliss overwhelms you to the point where you can't tell the difference between pleasure and pain?"

CHAPTER SIXTEEN

Damon

Sophia's head lolled to the side as she closed her eyes, lost in the thoughts I'd whispered into her ear.

As her pussy quivered around the humming dildo, her ass clenched around my cock.

Fuck. I wasn't sure how long I'd last.

My mind raged with relentless driving, urges to pound into her, to lose myself in her until all of the pent-up need inside me released.

Going so long without her and not fucking her in the Morelli Mansion had tested my strength.

When she'd dropped to her knees with the urge to suck me off, it felt like a small mercy from heaven. It was the only reason I lasted this long.

However, my willpower was still questionable. Especially with the vibrations of the toy sitting right up against my cock and the muscles of Sophia's tight ass squeezing the hell out of me.

"You know what I want. You've always known." Her erratic pants grew into whimpers as she gyrated her hips.

"What makes you so sure? I broke your trust before."

She arched her neck, a grimace of needy agony on her features. "Please. This waiting, wanting."

"Answer me."

"What do you want me to say? I know you won't ever take it beyond what I can handle."

"How do you know?" I had to hear her tell me I fixed the mess I made of us.

"Why are you so determined for me to say it?"

"Because I need to know you believe it."

She tossed her head back and forth. "You make no sense. How do you know I'm telling the truth if I say it?"

"You don't lie. Not to me. You won't lie to me even if it breaks your heart."

Tears poured from her eyes. "You're such an asshole. You do know this?"

"I know." I kissed the back of her head and shifted us forward, gritting my teeth against the waves of sensation bombarding my cock. "Tell me, My Sophia."

She hiccupped and then whispered, "I trust

you. I always have, even when I didn't want to. Why do you think I fought you so hard?"

"Then you agree there is no getting out of this for either of us."

"I thought we established this. You're the one who needed to catch up." She pushed her ass against me and then gasped when I adjusted the vibrator to one of the higher settings. "Will you stop talking and move? I'm dying here."

Setting a slow and steady pace, I gave her time to adjust to the dual sensation pulsing in her body.

Who the fuck was I kidding?

I needed the time, too. My balls ached, wanting so desperately to fuck Sophia as if I were a madman.

I closed my eyes, breathing through the exquisite pleasure of her body. There was absolutely nothing comparable to her scent, feel, or heat.

Whimpers and moans bubbled up from her throat, and she cried out, "Damon, help me. Too slow, faster. Please."

Her nails pressed against the cross where she was bound.

Increasing the speed of my hips, I slid two fingers along her swollen, sensitive clit. I stroked it, making her buck against me, and then, when she least expected, I pinched the bundle of nerves between my knuckles.

Her entire body went rigid, her pussy clamping down on the rubber cock lodged inside her, and her ass squeezing my dick in a vise grip.

Her cries of release obliterated what remained of my control, and the animal inside me surged forward. I pulled out and surged back in, allowing my primal need to take over.

I pounded into her, loving the sounds of her sobs and shouts. She thrashed and gasped, whimpered and moaned.

This was fucking heaven.

"Oh God, Damon," she called out the instant my orgasm washed through me, indicating she flew over into another release with me.

I pumped hard and hot into her, feeling as if this ride would never end. Losing myself in her was mind-blowing and beyond anything I'd ever experienced before.

"Say it," I ordered as my head dropped against the back of her neck, and my breath came out in short pants.

"S-say what?"

I bit her shoulder. "You know, exactly, what I want to hear."

"You say it."

So fucking stubborn.

"I love you, Sophia."

"Ditto." The smirk she shot me over her shoulder had me wanting to smack her ass.

But that would require moving, and I wasn't quite ready for that.

"I want the words."

"I love you."

I inhaled deep, letting her words soak in. It felt like a balm to my soul.

"Even when you broke my heart, I never stopped loving you."

I'd known this. I'd always known this.

"I'll make it up to you."

This was a soul-deep promise. Sophia deserved so much better than what I'd given her.

She trusted me when no one else would have given me the time of day.

Her not using the safeword before and today was to show she believed in me so much that I'd never intentionally put her in harm's way.

"It's in the past. We move forward. Leave it there."

"If that's what you want. Let's clean up." I reluctantly pulled from her body, hearing a whimper from her lips as the tip of my cock cleared the puckered opening.

Moving to the sink, I soaked a warm cloth, brought it back, and cleaned Sophia. Then I freed her legs and arms and slowly lowered her from the cross. Leaning her against a nearby lounging bench, I cared for her back, applying a salve to her skin. All the while, I massaged her muscles to keep them from cramping.

Once finished, I wrapped a blanket around her, carried her to the couch in the corner of the room, and sat down with her on my lap.

This woman was mine. But first, I'd have to get her to accept it.

I wanted marriage, a future, a family.

And we needed to change her damn safeword.

She sighed, fluttering her eyes closed.

She was so fucking beautiful, absolute perfection, and a complete pain in my ass.

"I know what you're thinking." She murmured with her head tucked against my chest.

"What am I thinking?"

She lifted her head and smiled. "That I'm a pain in the ass since I don't give you what you want when you want it."

How the fuck had she known that?

"Technically, only a few minutes ago, I was the pain in your ass."

"Very funny. I'm serious. You push me, I'll

push right back. It's not me being a brat. It's me forcing you to be honest about your feelings."

I lifted her chin and met her sleepy gaze. "Believe me. I know this. I'll be eighty years old, and you'll still be riding my ass about something."

"Are you assuming I will live with you when you're eighty?"

"You're marrying me, so there isn't any other place you'll live."

"Are we back to that again?" She shifted, trying to sit up.

"It's a given, Sophia. There's no one else for either of us."

"That may be true, but I'm not doing anything unless you ask me. I decide my future. I will stay in my apartment, and you can live in your ice palace." The stubborn set of her jaw annoyed me at times.

"Are you still afraid of marriage?"

"No. I only want the option to say yes or no."

"So you would say yes if I asked?"

"Propose and find out."

I flipped her onto her back, pressing her into the couch cushions, and loomed over her.

"I should punish you for being so stubborn."

A crease formed between Sophia's brows, and the humor disappeared from her face. She turned her head to the side and sniffed the air.

"Do you smell that?"

Within seconds of her asking, the scent hit my nostrils.

I jerked Sophia up. "Get dressed. Something is absolutely burning. We need to get out of here."

Then I looked over to the pile of clothes on the chair. Fuck, if there was a fire, Sophia couldn't wear what she had on before. I rushed to one of the cabinets the club kept stocked in each playroom for aftercare.

Opening it, I scanned the contents and pulled out a pair of lounge pants and a shirt, tossing them to Sophia. "Put this on over your other clothes. If there is a fire, it will protect you until we get outside."

Barely a minute later, the fire alarm sounded, and the lights went out.

"We have to move." Sophia urged. "Whatever's happening, it's on this side of the building. The smoke is getting heavier. If the sprinklers go off, we won't be able to see anything. It also means we are in the area of the fire. Sprinklers don't go off in the entire building, only in triggered areas."

"How do you know anything about sprinklers?" I grabbed two blankets and draped them over Sophia and me for added cover.

"I like investigation shows. I learned a few things."

"Well, arson investigator, we must get out of here."

When I opened the door, a massive black cloud of smoke billowed into the room. We both coughed and then covered our mouths.

We stepped out of the room into darkness. A red arrow on the ground at the far end of the corridor indicated the emergency exit was in that direction.

We slowly worked our way down the hallway. Knowing it was my duty to ensure people got out, I opened various playrooms, checking they were empty. Luckily, none so far were occupied.

Just as we reached the arrow, a boom rocked the building.

"Damon." Sophia grabbed hold of me.

"I'm here."

A surge of heat pushed through from the side where we'd just left, and relief washed over me. In the next second, the sprinklers triggered.

"See. I told you."

"Sophia, I don't care about sprinklers. Move. There's the exit."

Instead of waiting for her to follow directions, I threw her over my shoulder and ran, not putting her down until we reached the outside.

"What the hell, Damon." Her incredulous glare had me pulling her to me and holding her tight.

I turned to see fire blooming through the roof of the kitchen section of the club.

The private member rooms were right near there.

I closed my eyes and kissed the top of Sophia's head. I'd gotten her out of danger.

Finally, I'd done something right with her.

"Pierce, we have a problem." Ventana came up from behind me.

Ash covered his face, and the worry etched across his features wasn't something I'd ever seen before.

"What do you need me to do?"

"There are too many people still missing. I can't check every area alone. I need help. You know the building."

"Where?"

"The observation rooms and submissives' quarters."

Without thinking, I nodded, grabbed the flashlight in his hand, and rushed inside.

I could hear Sophia shouting at me, but I knew what I had to do.

My heart pounded as every possible worst-case scenario passed through my head. A fire in a club like this could be disastrous. So many people were in compromising situations.

Dear God, if a complicated bondage configuration was in play, there wasn't any way to unravel it quickly. The only options were industrial scissors, and that still took minutes. Minutes we more than likely didn't have.

I turned a corner near the observation room and heard a scream.

"Get me down. Please. Hurry."

Running in that direction, I found a submissive bound to a Saint Andrew's Cross. Two people worked to release her arms from the cuffs that were holding them in place.

Not asking permission from the men standing before, I pushed them to the side and quickly released the tiny woman from the straps.

These idiots required more training.

"Why the fuck are you using equipment meant for more experienced Doms?"

That's when my attention homed in on the submissive. I studied her long blonde hair, petite frame, and dark brown eyes. Oh shit. This was bad.

Lenora.

She was not only a club submissive but Master Jeremy's wife. There was no way in hell he would have abandoned her.

I tucked my head under Lenora's arm and caught her around the waist before lowering her.

"We were here for the demonstration," one of the men explained.

"Where is Master Jeremy?"

"We don't know. He was right there next to her. Then the room filled with smoke, and the lights went out."

Worry crept in when I glanced down at Lenora, who'd grown quiet. Her eyes were closed, making me believe smoke inhalation had overcome her.

"Take her out of here." I handed her to the larger of the guys. "Follow the hallway to the left and make sure the medical staff checks her out. I am going to see if I can find Master Jeremy."

I scooted around the stage and searched the preparation areas without seeing if they listened. The beam from the flashlight only gave me a limited view of the area. I scanned the room and then caught the shadow of a shoe.

Pushing furniture out of the way, I reached the body. Identifying it was Jeremy, in a state of complete unconsciousness, I checked his vitals and then hauled him over my shoulder.

Jesus, he was a hell of a lot heavier than he looked. I staggered a bit under his weight and then managed to make it out in time to see four fire engines arrive.

A medic took hold of Jeremy from my hands, and without thought, I went in search of Sophia.

Where the hell was she?

Through the haze of smoke and people, I caught sight of Clark.

Running in his direction, I asked, "Where's Sophia?"

He turned toward a group of people crowded in a circle and pointed and just as fast dropped his arm, a frown sliding over his features.

"The last time I saw her. She was over there, accounting for everyone against the admission log."

Everything inside me clenched when I couldn't spot Lizzy.

As if sensing my thoughts, Clark asked, "You don't think she went inside to find Lizzy?"

CHAPTER SEVENTEEN
Sophia

WHERE WERE LIZZY and Foster?

I scanned the crowds gathered in various areas outside of Violent Delights, trying to make out the different facial features of the people around me.

The air was thick with a sulfuric scent brought on by the continuing blaze running rampant in the building, making my eyes burn and easily breathing was a hard task to accomplish.

CLARK ORDERED EVERYONE to check in with me during the headcount process. He had tasked me to keep me from running after Damon when he sprinted into the building to play the hero.

Lizzy and Foster were supposed to be out here. So why couldn't I find them, and why hadn't they followed directions and checked in?

Worry crept in as I searched for Damon, too.

This whole disaster made no damn sense.

In all the years of the club, why today? What could have happened to cause this fire?

A loud crackle sounded in the distance, followed by an explosion. Out of instinct, I ducked, covering my head with my hands, and crouched near a parked car.

Debris flew into the air, but fortunately, it was in the opposite direction of where everyone gathered.

My heart thumped into my chest as I stood and realized the fire shot high from the area where Damon and I were only an hour earlier.

I continued to search my way through different groups, not seeing any signs of Lizzy or Foster.

I spotted a house submissive that I recognized and ran toward her. "Milly, have you seen Foster? He was with my sister. I can't find either of them."

Milly's eyes widened, and her face drained of color. "Oh, no. This is bad."

"What? Tell me where they are."

"They were in the costume room trying on different outfits."

"Why is that bad?"

"The only way to access that part of the club is through the kitchen or the accessway in the performance rooms."

My hands shook. That was the area where the explosion just came from.

"What if they're still in there? I have to find out."

"Are you crazy?" Milly grabbed my arm. "Master Damon will kill me if I let anything happen to you."

"That's my sister. I brought her here. I'm responsible for her. I'm going in no matter what you say. Damon doesn't have a choice."

"Please don't do this." She searched around her as if she could find someone to keep me from following through with my plan. "It's dangerous."

"Do you have siblings?"

"Two younger brothers and one older sister."

"Wouldn't you do everything possible to ensure they were safe in this situation?"

Her face dropped in resignation, and she pointed to a location over my shoulder. "There is a pathway along the right side of the building. It will lead you around the back and away from the location of the fire. Please be careful."

"Thank you." I hugged her and sprinted in the direction she said to follow.

Even with the acidic mix of wood and plastic, and God knew what scents of the various burned building materials filled the air, this side of the massive club seemed safer than where I'd just left. At least for now, anyway.

As the crackling of wood splintering and the roaring of the fire continued, I navigated the zigzag walkway.

Once I reached the maintenance side of the club, I paused, realizing this was where the employees parked and how another world existed back here. The glitz and glamour of Violent Delights were all in front, but this took me behind the scenes.

Five dumpsters with distinct labels sat on the far end of a brick wall enclosure, and there was at least a fifty-foot gap between where the parking area started and the building. That could be where the trucks came in with all the deliveries of supplies.

I followed the roof line as something in my gut told me Lizzy's instinct would be to go higher if trapped in any building.

She was a Morelli woman.

She wasn't one to wait for rescue.

In the distance, a handful of people were in the area Milly described as the section designated as the costume room.

Please, Lizzy, be among that group.

Nausea churned in my belly as a pang of fear

filled my mind.

What would I do if she wasn't there? How would I explain this?

Guilt washed over me. I shouldn't have left Lizzy.

I had to find her. I was responsible for her. It was because of me that she came here.

I knew this wasn't the place for her from the beginning. Why hadn't I made her understand she wasn't ready? I'd thrown her into the deep end instead of easing her into the world of kink.

My lips trembled as logic seeped in.

No one could have stopped Lizzy if she set her mind to something.

If I'd turned her down, she would have gone to Lucian. More than likely, he would have said to come back when she was older, which meant she'd find another, more dangerous avenue to explore the lifestyle.

Sirens wailed in the distance, warning of the fire department's impending arrival. At the same time, another blast cracked through the building, and fire shot into the air.

Jesus. Could a gas main have exploded?

That was when I heard, "Sophia. Sophia. Is that you? Over here."

"Lizzy?" I looked in the direction where I saw

the people on the roof.

I charged over, my heart beating into my ears.

I called out again, this time at the top of my lungs, "Lizzy, over here. It's Sophia."

As I neared, I noticed someone holding an injured woman against their shoulder and Lizzy and Foster waving me toward them.

"Oh my God, Sophia. You have no idea how happy I am to see you." Lizzy's hoarse voice told me either her throat was raw from screaming or smoke. "The ladder collapsed just as we pulled Tammy up here."

That must be the girl who couldn't put any weight on her foot.

I scanned near her, trying to find any flat area where maintenance would use to access equipment. "We have to get you down. I'm not sure if the roof is safe. Do you see any utility stairwells?"

I'd used so many of them to escape through during fashion shows. There had to be some here.

"There is an emergency exit near the heating and cooling shaft about fifty feet away. The maintenance crew has their offices near there," someone shouted. "If we hurry, we could make it there."

My stomach dropped as I looked toward the area where he gestured. Going in that direction meant we would bring everyone closer to the fire.

There was no choice.

"I'll meet you there."

Less than two minutes later, I reached the area the guy directed us to. I pulled the metal door handle, but it wouldn't budge.

Panic set it. I yanked on it again, and this time it slightly shifted.

The heat in the area may be affecting the door. Pulling with all my strength, it finally opened, and a blast of warm air cascaded over me.

Ignoring the fear running through my system in full force, I pulled out my phone from my pocket, turned on the light, and used it to guide me toward the stairs.

Shit, if anyone expected to use this as an emergency exit, shouldn't the stairs be closer to the doors?

I needed to discuss this with Lucian. What a terrible fucking design. Whoever he hired needed a punch in the face or a kick in the head, which was more like it.

Why the fuck was I thinking about building layouts when I needed to get to Lizzy?

Pushing my rambling thoughts back, I turned a corner to find two men holding the woman I assumed was Tammy down the stairs. There was blood seeping from a wound on her face.

"Follow that hallway to the left. It will take you directly out," I directed the group. "Don't stay near the building. Go into the parking lot."

As I took the first step, I yelled to the men, "Where are Lizzy and Foster?"

"They were right behind us. Anderson tripped in the rush to get down, so they are helping him."

A crash echoed through the walls near me, and I took two steps up at a time.

As I reached the second landing, I saw Lizzy and Foster with Anderson between them. Anderson had his leg bent, and he hobbled down on one foot.

Pain etched his face, telling me there was no way we would get down fast.

Not with the man's size and injury.

When Lizzy's eyes connected with mine, relief washed through them. "Sophia, I knew you'd come. You're always there for me."

Her words hit me in the gut. No matter what, I'd be there for her.

Tears streamed down her face, and I could tell panic welled up inside her. The only way to keep her calm was to distract her.

Even when we were little, if I talked to her about anything nonsensical, she wouldn't focus on whatever chaos churned around us.

I rushed toward them. "Why didn't you bring Tammy down, and the two big guys handle Anderson?"

"Because we didn't realize how badly Anderson was hurt until he tried to put weight on his leg and fell." Lizzy stumbled under Anderson's weight when he shifted to adjust his hold on Lizzy's shoulder.

"I think I broke it," Anderson gritted out. "I was trying to keep the door from locking us out. The auto locks will engage if anyone accesses the roof without a keycard, and I lost mine when the ladder broke."

"Why the roof and not an emergency exit?"

"I don't know Sophia. Let me think. There was an explosion and a fire. We couldn't see, and roof access was the first thing near us." The annoyance on Lizzy's face would have been comical in any other situation.

"Okay, okay. Sorry. Don't be so testy."

"This is not testy. This is scared."

I sighed, "I'll get you out."

"I know you will."

I moved in next to Lizzy, tucked my head under Anderson's arm, and settled some of his weight onto me.

"I feel like a wimp."

Anderson decided to chime in on our conversation. "Technically, I'm the wimp since two women and my best bud are carrying me down the stairs in a fire, and I'm the certified volunteer fireman."

"Really?" I couldn't hide the surprise in my voice.

"Yep," Anderson shook his head. "Embarrassing isn't even the word for this."

"Let's move."

With Lizzy and me on one side of Anderson and Foster on the other, we slowly worked our way down.

We'd barely gone four steps when sweat beaded my face.

I wasn't sure if it was the anxiety of going down so many steps or the temperature had increased.

"I think the fire is getting closer. It's hotter than hell in here." Foster blew out a deep breath.

Okay, I wasn't the only one who felt the heat.

"Lizzy, if we survive this," Foster added. "I'm taking you to see how real fashion school students party."

"I'll hold you to it. But let's do something low-key first. I don't think my nerves can take anything adventurous for a little while."

"You'll change your mind once you start Abbott's class next week," Anderson muttered.

"You're a firefighter and—" I coughed as smoke filled the space around us. "Y-you're in school with her?"

"All of us are," Foster said, taking more of Anderson's weight as we reached a landing and had to turn. "Not the firefighter part, just the school part."

"And you never met until tonight?"

"The school is big," Lizzy tried to defend herself.

"No, that's not true." Anderson said, "We haven't met because Lizzy hangs out with the wrong crowd."

"I'll give you that." Lizzy agreed. "I'm over the assholes."

Was this the reason she kept coming home? Were her friends at school complete jerks, and it wasn't a guy problem at all?

"What year are you two?"

"Foster is a second-year like me," Lizzy answered, then tilted her head toward Anderson. "He's a third."

Maybe bringing her here hadn't been a bad idea after all. She found friends in some warped sort of way.

"Now it makes sense why so many of you were in this area together."

"Do you mean the costume room or a kink club?" Lizzy barely asked her silly question before she screamed as a beam crashed through the ceiling where we were standing only a few seconds earlier.

We all ducked, and I heard a pained grunt from Anderson.

"No more talking. We have to move."

"I can't move any faster. Only one working leg, remember?" Anderson's voice had my worry ratcheting up.

"Okay, we can do this. We are going to try to carry you down. You hang on to us and lift both legs. Don't help. This whole experience won't be comfortable, but it's better than the alternative."

"I hear you." Anderson closed his eyes as if in agony, and I glanced down at his foot, seeing the angle wasn't quite right.

"Ready," I asked.

They all nodded.

Just as we shifted to move, Damon rushed up the stairs. "Sophia, are you out of your mind?"

Seeing him almost brought tears to my eyes. He made it out of the building. He was safe.

No, he came back in for me.

"Damon, what are you doing here?"

"That's the question I need to ask you. You were supposed to stay where I left you."

Where he left me? I glared at him.

"Can we do this later? We're busy at the moment?" Lizzy shifted her body, ready to lift Anderson." We need to get Anderson out of here."

"Let me take him." He pushed Lizzy and me out of the way. "The two of you get outside. Foster and I will bring Anderson down."

"We all stay together." He would not send me away.

"For God's sake, listen to me." Damon's exasperation annoyed the hell out of me.

"You don't get to take over just because you're here now."

"Have it your way." He nodded in Foster's direction, and they rose together, lifting Anderson with a hand under the shoulders and behind the knee.

As we all rushed down the stairs, Anderson observed, "You aren't like any submissive I've ever encountered. I'm not sure how to label you."

"You don't even know the half of it," Damon muttered. "She's a brat on the best of days.

Others, I have yet to figure out."

"Funny."

We reached the ground level right as a blast shook the building. Drywall and debris fell all around us, and visibility was almost non-existent.

A dim glow down the hall was the only indicator that the exit doors were in that direction. I realized somewhere along the way, I'd dropped my phone.

At this point, it no longer mattered. I had no plans to go back and look for it.

We turned the corner when Clark found us with some of his security team.

"You're a hardheaded jackass, Pierce. At least wait for backup before charging in." He motioned with his head for his team to grab Anderson.

"Help. Please Help. I'm stuck in here." The faint cry sent a chill down my spine, making everyone freeze.

Clark and Damon shared some unsaid communication, nodded, and then ran down the hallway we'd come from.

I tried to follow, but Foster held me back by the waist and then pulled me out into the open night. "Oh, hell no. You are too important to Lizzy and Master Damon."

I thrashed and pushed against Foster's hand.

The crisp, clean air should have been refreshing after being in the smoke for so long, but everything inside me felt crushed and in pain.

"Let me go. You don't understand. Damon won't listen to anyone except me. He's hardheaded."

"So are you, Sophia." Lizzy took hold of my wrists. "Breathe. I need you to breathe."

As if on cue, paramedics neared, covered us in a blanket, and surrounded us. They blocked my view, and no matter how hard I tried, they were determined to keep me from escaping the questions and screenings.

The EMT placed an oxygen mask on my face, which I kept batting away until Lizzy held it against me. "You'll keep this on, or I'll tape it to your head."

My attention snapped to her. "I can't lose him. Don't you see? We're finally figuring things out."

"It is going to be fine." Her words barely left her lips as an explosion burst through the roof in front of us.

Then, at the door, I saw Clark carrying a woman in his hands, but no one else came out behind him.

Oh, God. No. This wasn't happening. No. This wasn't fucking happening.

CHAPTER EIGHTEEN
Damon

I OPENED MY eyes as searing pain shot through the back of my head and radiated more down my leg. I tried to sit up but dropped back down when I realized something lay across my lower body, keeping me from moving. Shifting my arms, I dislodged whatever debris sat on my upper body. My arms hurt like a motherfucker, but at least I hadn't broken them.

Now, my foot, who knew? Or maybe it was my leg. At this point, with whatever fell through the ceiling and nearly crushed me, I was lucky to be alive.

But how the fuck had I gotten here? None of it made sense.

Slowly, images popped forward.

The fire. Sophia.

Panic settled in my chest. No, I remember her getting out.

I winched. My head hurt as if needles pierced

into my ears.

The moment I tried to take a deep breath, I choked on the smoke and coughed uncontrollably.

Fuck me. Where the fuck was my mask?

I know I had one on my face. Clark gave me one.

I saw flashes of running into the building with Clark and searching for a woman crying out for help. We found a server who fell during the evacuation and got caught under falling debris.

As if it were a tidal wave, my memory cleared.

Clark and I barely managed to pull the server free when a small explosion started.

The fucking bar stockroom. The source of the detonation. It had to be.

They were only a few rooms away from us. The initially small burst sounded more like champagne bottles uncorking.

I guessed the fire decided to have a drink or three and couldn't hold its liquor.

It still didn't make sense why I was here and not outside. After pulling the server free, everything seemed fuzzy. I remembered telling Ventana to go and that I'd follow. Now I was here.

Was there something else that blew up?

"Ventana, are you in here?" I shouted and

immediately regretted it as I broke out into another wave of uncontrollable coughing, and the pounding in my head intensified into the equivalent of knives jabbing into my skull.

Closing my eyes, I covered my face with my hands and willed the pain to ease.

There wasn't any point in taking deep breaths. The smoky air around me kept thickening, making my throat burn as if I were drinking down a bottle of acid.

I blinked a few times, and the haze cleared from my eye. But it made no difference. The room was still shrouded, mostly in darkness.

The only light source came from the emergency exit lights in a distant hallway. An area of the room I could not reach any time soon.

I stared up at the cracked ceiling and exposed beams above me that once held the second story of the club. How much more damage could it take before the whole thing collapsed and crushed me?

Was this the legacy I'd leave behind? Not my architecture or contributions to design, but dying in a kink club.

I guessed it served me right for everything I'd done in my life.

Plus, this was where I'd met Maria, and because of me and my neglect in seeing her obsession with me, her inability to accept that I could never love her and that she'd killed herself.

This could be an eye for an eye situation.

But then again, I met my Sophia here—the woman who made me feel more than sexual attraction. She brought out a side of me I'd never known existed.

I winched as a wave of dizziness rushed through my head.

"If this is your version of knocking some sense into me. I believe we are teetering on the side of overkill," I said into the void, knowing the only one I could talk to was the Almighty, who probably wasn't fond of me.

Then, I asked, "Was bringing Sophia into my life and snatching her away in this manner a punishment for me and my family's crimes?"

Not truly expecting a response, I continued.

"I won't deny it. Sophia deserves so much better than me. I'm not a good man. I own this. However, she is a good person. Please don't make her suffer after I'm gone. Find her someone worthy."

The smoke around grew denser, and I expected to pass out soon as the ability to take in small sips of air grew harder and harder.

My mind drifted with images of Sophia, her smile, her eyes. I could almost hear her call my name.

Wait. That was her calling my name.

"Sophia?" I croaked out, my throat barely cooperating with the blades piercing the inside of my neck.

A beam of light shined across my face, blinding me in the dark and reigniting the pounding in the back of my mind that had only slightly settled.

Was I imagining things as a symptom of traumatic brain injury?

Or did my desperate need to be around her conjure her voice?

"Damon. Oh God. Damon. I'm coming."

There it was again. I'd rather pass out or something than live with this torture until my ultimate demise.

Suddenly, my head lifted, and soft hands cradled my face, brushing my hair from my forehead.

That touch, her smell—no, this couldn't be happening.

When a mask covered my nose and mouth, panic welled up inside me. I reached up, and my hands closed around arms I'd recognize anywhere.

No, no, no.

She was supposed to stay outside where she was safe and away from the fire, with no chance of a single flame hurting her.

Why wouldn't she ever fucking listen? Why the fuck hadn't Clark stopped her?

He'd done everything possible to keep me from her but decided to let her run into a burning building.

My hold on her forearms tightened, homing in on her mask-covered face. Recognizing her eyes, and then dread shot through me.

"Go, now. This roof will collapse any minute."

As if not hearing me, she said, "I have to figure out a way to get you out."

The determination in the voice made it seem as if there were no other possibilities. But I knew the truth. I wasn't getting out of here.

"Sophia, what are you doing here?"

"Isn't it obvious? Rescuing you." She tucked something soft under my neck and head, easing some of my discomfort, shifted from under me, and then rose, picking up the large searchlight she'd set on the floor and attaching it to her hip.

I tried to grab hold of her, but I realized my grip wasn't as firm as I believed.

"You need to leave right this second."

"Maybe in a few seconds, if not this one. Is that the perfect compromise?" The scraping of furniture on the ground reached my ears. "Then you can come with me, too."

"That's not a compromise." I clenched my fists, hating how weak and useless I felt. "God knows what is pinning me to the floor, and I'm positive I broke or shattered my foot. How the fuck am I coming with you?"

"Watch and see."

Was she out of her mind?

"I'm ordering you to leave."

"You're in no position to order me to do anything."

I resisted the urge to grit my teeth, knowing I'd regret it. "Want to tell me what's keeping me locked in place."

"It's fitting considering our escapade from earlier in the evening." I heard tearing and a screech as if she was grinding something.

"No need for the dramatic pause."

"Hold on. Let me do this, and I'll tell you." She muttered under her breath as she wrapped some fabric or rope on the contraption holding me down.

Once finished, she exhaled and said, "It's a

Saint Andrew's Cross and its weight-bearing anchor beam. It fell through one of the second-floor playrooms."

Of all the things to fall on me, fabulous.

"I think once I get this piece of the bar under the long section, I can shimmy it up."

"Do you realize how heavy that is?"

"Yes, I do. I just moved it."

A series of pops came from the storage area, and I only dreaded what might happen next.

"Sophia, run. Please, run."

"I am not leaving you. Do you think I came in here and went through all this effort to return empty-handed?"

"I'm trying to protect you. Any second, there is going to be an explosion. Those tiny bursts you're hearing are coming from the bar stockroom."

"We know how things go when you protect me. I'm handling this my way."

"For Christ's sake. Will you listen to me for once? I am fucking ordering you to leave me here and get out right this instant? Do you hear me?"

"Listen up." Suddenly, she appeared two inches from my face, her eyes ablaze with fury. "You don't get to tell me what to do? I am not losing you. Do you hear me?"

"This is a command, as your Dom."

Tears streamed down her cheeks. "I have to get this off you. I almost have it figured out. Let me try this. Please."

I cupped her cheek, brushing the dampness from her skin. "There is no time. You will not die because of me."

Another woman would not lose her life because of my negligence. This woman was my everything, the only one to break open my heart and make it possible for me to love.

Why couldn't she see that she had to get out of here? She had to live for my death to mean something.

"I am not Maria. You will not take on some guilt that isn't yours to carry. Do you hear me?"

"I never said you were."

She leaned closer, bringing us nose to nose. "I see it in your eyes. I know you, Damon Pierce. I fucking know you."

"Leave." Unable to resist, I fisted her hair.

"No."

"You don't get to say no. I'm your Dom, and it is an order. Get out."

"Not happening, so get over it."

"This isn't the time to play brat. You aren't safe. I'm ending it. Go if you love me."

She jerked as if I'd slapped her with my words. Hurt washed over her features. Immediately I felt like an asshole, but I'd use anything in my arsenal to get her out of there.

"Don't use my love against me."

"Go." I drew her forehead to mine. "I love you, Sophia. Please do this for me."

Lifting up slightly, she held my gaze. Her lips trembled as if accepting the situation, and she leaned down to kiss me.

My heart shattered knowing this would be the last time I'd ever feel her mouth pressed to mine, but also seeing she'd have a long life and future.

When she pulled back, she continued to hold my gaze and stood. She took three steps backward, glanced to her side, her lips trembling, and then returned her focus to me.

All of a sudden, a coolness washed over her features before a crease formed between her brows, and with a firm set to her jaw, she whispered, "Marriage."

"You can't be serious." I pushed up with my arms, ignoring the pain I caused in my head and body. "Sophia, this isn't a scene. You promised to leave."

She cocked a hand on her hip. "I made no such promise. You pulled the Dom on me. I'm using my safeword. Deal with it."

"Dammit, Sophia."

Ignoring me, she shifted her attention to push more of the bar in my direction. My heartbeat sped up, and a chill slid down my back despite the heat building in the room when everything grew quiet outside of the periodic hiss and pop every few seconds in the distance.

"Over here," she said.

I barely caught the shadow of light silhouetting her before I noticed she planned to push a loose ten-foot stabilizer beam down from the ceiling.

"Are you out of your fucking mind?" The heavy wood crashed down before I finished my question.

It landed on whatever contraption Sophia created, and the section securing my thighs and waist to the ground jerked up, releasing all the pressure on my lower body and flooding my system with blood and sensations.

I fell back, rolling to my side. I could barely breathe. Stars appeared behind my eyes as dizziness overwhelmed me and nausea filled my stomach.

The agony of my shattered foot radiated through me in each wave of my nerves firing to life. All the movement only added to the overwhelming pounding in my head.

"Sophia," I gasped out. "I'm not sure that was a good idea."

A few curses and grunts later, Sophia appeared. "Please forgive me. I have to pull you out from under there. I don't know how long that will hold."

Unable to focus on anything but the misery of the chaos that was my body, I nodded.

Sophia moved behind me, hooked her arms under mine, and lifted me. "On the count of three, I'm going to pull. Please don't hate me. There isn't much time."

The panic in her voice cleared a fraction of the haze in my mind and made me realize she'd kept her anxiety about the situation from me.

"I could never hate you. Do what you have to do." I latched my hands onto her forearms and waited.

"One, two, three." She clenched her teeth and pulled.

I cried out as my damaged foot hit the wood, she yanked me through, but somehow, she managed to bring all of me out in one try.

She fell onto her bottom with me on top of her.

She panted, unable to do more than take in small sips of air with the smoke pressing down on us. "Damon, I feel so tired."

Adrenaline surged through me, hearing the dreamy way she made her statement. Turning to look at her, I immediately sat up, regardless of the mess that was my leg and foot.

She no longer wore her mask, and color had drained from her face. Her eyelids fluttered as if they were too heavy to keep open.

"So tired," she repeated.

No, I wouldn't lose her now. Not after all she risked for me.

"Sophia. You didn't come all this way to let the fire win. Come on. Help me up."

I tugged the mask from my face, put it on her, and then used my torn shirt to make a makeshift mask for me. Grabbing the light from Sophia, I searched around me and found a turned over chair.

It would have to work as a crutch.

A crackle rang through the room, and a moment later, the ceiling fell through on the spot I was in only seconds ago.

Shifting my attention to her, we stared at each other. Sophia saved my life with no time to spare.

"I told you I'd get you out."

"You did."

"We have to move. There isn't any more time. I only had fifteen minutes. I went over."

"What do you mean you went over? By how much?"

"Ten minutes." She stood a bit shaky, tucked her head under my shoulder, and hoisted me up as I used the chair to help me on my non-injured side.

Clenching my jaw, I ignored the lightheadedness and said, "You don't ever fucking listen."

"Can we talk about this later? There are other priorities." She shifted me, and my ability to focus vanished.

"Sophia, I think I'm about to pass out." My one good leg grew weak.

Sophia shoved me onto the seat. "Passed out or not. I will drag you on this chair. We are getting out of here."

Right before I lost consciousness, someone shouted, "Ms. Morelli. Ms. Morelli. Are you in here? It's the fire department."

CHAPTER NINETEEN

Sophia

"IF ONE MORE person tells me they are going to have me checked out by some specialist for minor smoke inhalation, I am throwing you all out of this room." I glared at my family, who occupied nearly all the space in my hospital room.

What was the point of being admitted for observation to recover from a traumatic event if no one allowed me to fucking recover?

"Your color is off. I'm calling in Doctor Patterson," Lucian stated.

Before I could respond, Leo said, "She's the best in the field. Call her in."

Oh, for the love of God.

"I am fine. I only need rest. How many times do I need to emphasize this?"

"I know what the fire department said. You were in there double what they said was safe. It's better to err on the side of caution." Lucian glared at me.

"I had more tests than the average person gets. They are all clear. Why are we having this conversation again?"

"No, have it again. These discussions are amusing." Carter laughed. "It's like those old-school record players skipping, and the song repeats. Don't you agree?"

He leaned over to nod at Tiernan, who stood near him with his wife Bianca.

"This is more entertainment than I expected when I heard about the fire."

Lucian shifted his attention to him. "Shouldn't the two of you be on a different continent?"

I seriously needed some space.

It felt like a Morelli convention, but instead of everyone gathering for a wedding, it was my possible imminent demise.

Carter, June, and Theo stood off on one side of the room with Tiernan and Bianca. They continued to make jokes and snicker.

My brothers were grown, married men acting like teenagers.

I loved them all, but why had they dropped everything to come here? They were so eager to get out of town after Eva's wedding. Shouldn't they be vacationing, saving the world, or buying art? Or on another continent, like Lucian asked?

Then Leo added his two cents, "Sophia, give in, and we will leave you alone. What harm will it do to see someone we bring in? Once Dr. Patterson checks you out, we promise to keep everyone away from you. We donate enough to her program that she'll jump at the chance to come see you."

Leo and Lucian were about to get a fist to the nose if they kept up with the lord of the hospital shit.

"Because I don't need you to bring in anyone. I'm fine. According to the doctor, I didn't need to stay the night. I'm only here because of you and busybody over there."

"That's why you need a second opinion. These docs can't know everything," Leo defended.

"Get out. Right now. Elaine, Haley. I promise I will kill them."

The two overbearing butthead's saving graces were their wives. Elaine and Haley seemed to know exactly when I was ready to jump out of bed and throat punch one of them and found a convenient way to pull them out of the room for a private conversation.

It's too bad they missed the mark this time.

"We are not leaving until we have a press

release written." Dad folded his arms across his chest and glowered at everyone who looked in his direction.

"Oh, for fuck's sake, Dad," Lucian exclaimed. "Sophia nearly dies, and that's your priority. We need to focus on her health right now."

"He's right. What's more important, your daughter or a press release?" Leo glared at Dad.

"The two of you are a disgrace to the Morelli family name. I'm protecting the family legacy since none of you are bothered enough to do it."

Of course, Dad only cared about his image. He'd rather rant and rave about Lucian's sex club and how to redeem the family in the court of public opinion.

"I have a headache. Can all of you leave?" I shot a pleading look in Mom's direction, who only gave me her calm Sarah Morelli face, not the no makeup, unguarded face from our breakfast.

But to my surprise, she set a hand on Dad's forearm and said, "It is better to work on the statement in private so no one can overhear the planning. Hospital staff aren't known for their discretion."

Dad scowled and opened his mouth as if to argue, then nodded. "At least you have half a brain. Unlike any of the ungrateful lot in this room. Where's Eva?"

"I told her to go home to her husband and newborn child while you lectured Lucian about his club. She listens to me because she knows I'm a grown-up." I crossed my arms, so done with everyone.

"Then where are the other two?" Dad posed the question as if he'd forgotten his other daughters' names, which I knew he hadn't.

He hadn't even realized three of his daughters left the room being too focused on his tirade.

"You mean Daphne and Lizzy?" asked Emerson, Daphne's husband. "They are running an errand for Sophia."

He leaned against a wall, looking inconspicuous and distant. And since that was his nature, everyone just accepted it. The last thing the Morellis could do was cast stones. Though given the chance, Dad loved to toss them at everyone to deflect blame for issues so no one would look at him.

Such was the Bryant Morelli way.

"What type of errand?" Lucian demanded, breaking into my musings.

Everyone, except Emerson turned their attention to me, awaiting an answer.

"None of your business."

"Come on, Sarah. I'm going home. I know when I'm not wanted." Dad didn't acknowledge me, and I shouldn't have expected otherwise.

Mom approached and kissed my forehead. "Get some rest."

I nodded.

Not two minutes after the parents left, Lizzy and Daphne strode into the room, heading straight for me with a note. However, Leo snatched it from my finger before I could take it.

"What is wrong with you? That was for me. I'm calling security." I pushed my covers down and readied to jump from the bed.

Lizzy pushed me down and crawled in next to me. "Stay."

"Why aren't they on your case? You were in the club with me?"

"Because I stayed outside once the explosions started, and you went inside to save your man."

I pursed my lips. "Oh."

Leo read the note and sighed.

"What does it say? Give it to me." Lucian snatched the paper from Leo's fingers and read. "At least one of you has common sense."

"Meaning?."

"Pierce said you are forbidden to see him until you are one hundred percent healed."

Forbidden. Okay, whatever. "Is that all it says?"

"No, but I'm not reading that out loud with any of these people in the room."

"Well, get them to leave. Oh, and you can go with them and leave the note behind."

"Just let us have someone check you over. What is the big deal?" There was a plea in his eyes he had never shown me before.

Then it hit me. Lucian was really worried and blamed himself for the fire.

Oh, Lucian. My big, bad, mean brother, who loved to act as if he terrorized the world. He carried so much on his shoulders. He couldn't honestly believe he was responsible for the mess that caused the fire.

But from his expression and the guilt I felt radiating off him in waves, it was exactly how he felt.

"It wasn't your fault. You can't blame yourself."

"Who do I blame then? If I hadn't agreed to the fire show, those idiots wouldn't have thought to bring in those tanks through the kitchen. I should have made sure security watched those morons like hawks."

"Everyone knows the shows load and unload

through the bay. Someone ignoring the rules isn't your fault."

"Of course, it is my fault. I own the club. I'm responsible for everyone there. Hundreds of people could have died. You and Lizzy could have died."

Leo spoke this time, "Your security did stop them when they tried to bring their tanks through the kitchen the first time. Your men warned them about open flames and the tanks."

"Then how the fuck did they get any of the tanks in the kitchen?" Lucian gripped the back of his neck. "I don't care. Those fuckers aren't working in the industry again. They aren't working anywhere again."

Deciding I needed to bring him back from the edge of murderous rage, I said, "You'll find out what happened in detail, deal with everything, rebuild. Please remember, this isn't your fault."

Elaine wrapped an arm around Lucian's waist. "She's right. You can't blame yourself for things that weren't in your control. First, we have to get the surveillance videos, and then we will see the truth of what happened."

He nodded. The resignation was still etched all over his face.

Deciding to give him a break and a little more

peace of mind, plus arguing about seeing a doctor and taking a few tests, was stupid in the grand scheme of things.

I said, "Call in your doc for a second opinion. I guess it wouldn't hurt to ensure everything was double okay with me."

He lifted his head, held my gaze for a few seconds, and nodded.

A few seconds later, Leo moved toward the door. "Come on, she wants to rest, and I think we've overstayed our welcome."

"Yeah, we did that an hour ago," Carter replied.

After everyone left, I read the note Lucian had placed at the bottom of my bed.

Sophia

Don't even think about leaving that bed to see me. I forbid you to come anywhere near me until you are one hundred percent healed.

If you break the rules, you will suffer the consequences. We know your favorite way of receiving punishment is via denial, or is that my favorite way of administering it? Whatever the answer, I'll come, and you won't.

-D

Oh, he thought he was so funny. He was the one with the shattered foot. What could he do to me?

✧ ✧ ✧

A LITTLE AFTER seven in the evening, I took the staff elevator down one floor and arrived on the level where Damon's room was.

As if Lizzy knew I planned to sneak out of my room no matter what anyone told me, an hour after she left with the family, she sent a text saying she hid a set of loungewear and a pair of slippers in a cabinet in my room so I wouldn't have to walk around the hospital in my gown and show all the patients my naked butt.

I had to give it to her for always thinking ahead and wanting to cover my butt, literally.

Now, I had to make it down two hallways without anyone noticing a patient walking around. And since Lucian and Leo decided to throw their weight around and announced their baby sister was in residence, I would need to be extra careful.

The only reason I managed to leave my room undetected was a group visiting the lady next door decided to go, and I hid amongst them. They'd given me strange looks, but then again, we were in a hospital, and people did weird things, so they accepted it.

A food delivery cart, at least five and a half feet tall, came down the corridor. I knew this was my chance to hide along the side of it. Stepping out as it passed, I followed its path until it turned, and I was almost to the area near Damon's room.

After another few minutes of careful maneuvering, I reached Damon's door and froze when I heard Clark's voice.

Shit. Shit. Shit.

He was going to rat me out to Lucian. Then I'd never hear the end of it, and by morning, I wouldn't doubt Lucian or Leo would have guards posted outside my door as if I were a criminal.

I could wait Clark out in one of the waiting rooms I passed. Yeah, that's what I'd do.

Pivoting, I motioned to go in the direction I came but stopped as soon as I heard.

"Don't even think about it. I saw you." I wasn't sure if Damon sounded amused or annoyed.

Wincing, I stayed in my spot.

"Sophia, come in here," Damon ordered.

There went my plans of escape. I wasn't getting out of seeing him.

With my shoulders back, I walked in as if I

hadn't a care in the world.

"Hi Clark, how's it going?"

He gave me a lift of the brow with a smirk. "I didn't die in a fire today, so I'd say well. Though I may be out of a job."

"I could always use you as a model in my upcoming fashion show."

Creating a few pieces specifically for men wasn't such a bad idea. I'd have to think more about it since I was under a time constraint with only a little over two months until Fashion Week. Maybe, if I worked fast, I could come up with a piece or two.

"I'll pass, but thank you." He shook his head and then shot Damon a look over my head.

"The offer is always open."

"Sophia," Damon said my name in a way that had a shiver sliding down my spine.

My eyes connected with his as that familiar energy surged between us. "Yes."

"Don't flirt with another Dom in my presence."

The hum of arousal fizzled out.

"Are you serious?" I scrunched my nose. "He's like a brother to me. And he's Lucian's friend. Nope. Not happening."

The humor on Clark's face told me he wasn't

offended by my response. "I concur. Besides, you're too much trouble."

"See—nothing to worry about. I'm not interested in Lucian's friends pool," I said, turning back to Damon.

His green irises locked with mine, and the tingle of need kindled back to life. "I'm in Lucian's friends pool, and it happened with us."

I hadn't known he was Lucian's anything when I'd set eyes on him. The only thing on my mind at the time was no other man drew me as Damon had, and if I didn't take a chance, I never would.

"It did." I licked my lips. "However, we know our introduction happened on a more organic level."

"That's an interesting way to put it." Clark chuckled. "I'm going to leave you to your submissive, Pierce."

Damon nodded, "We'll talk again soon."

Clark walked over to me, took my hand in his, and kissed the top of it. "I'll keep this among the three of us, Sophia. I'm sure you're in enough trouble already."

"Thanks, I think."

He shot me a grin and then walked out the door, closing it behind him.

"Come here," Damon commanded, snapping my attention to him.

Slowly, I stepped up on his good side, staying out of arm's reach. He may have a concussion and a broken foot, but his arms worked perfectly well.

As if sensing my thoughts, he said, "Afraid I'll turn you over my lap and spank you for ignoring my note?"

"What note?" I moved closer to him, my fingers skimmed across the blanket covering his non-injured leg.

"The one forbidding you to come see me."

"Oh, you mean that piece of paper Leo took from Daphne's hands? Once Leo and Lucian read it and I finally took a peek, I decided it was merely a suggestion."

"How did you come to that summation?"

"If it was a directive, you would have kept it private and sealed the message in an envelope. Since you left it open for anyone to read, I took it as sexy banter, nothing more."

An amused crease formed between his brows, and he shook his head. "Your logic is fascinating."

"Can I assume that's a good thing?"

"Yes, it's a very good thing. I'll never be bored with you in my life."

"I promise to keep things on the level of fashion shows and the occasional events, nothing too wild as the fire from earlier today."

"I've seen your fashion shows. They aren't tame by any measure."

"That's how I roll, Damon Pierce. Take it or leave it."

"Are we in a negotiation?"

I sat on the edge of his bed. "It does look that way."

"Are you my submissive, Sophia Morelli, or are you still exploring?" The way he asked that question kicked up my heartbeat and sent a shiver down my spine.

With him, I could be anything I wanted—always me in any form I deemed. I was safe, accepted, wanted.

He had to know I was his—his submissive, his brat, whatever he wanted to label it.

However, it didn't mean I wanted to stop discovering aspects about myself.

"I'm always exploring, Mr. Pierce," I said, seeing his green eyes go molten.

"Only, ever with me."

"Only, ever with you."

He smirked. "So you aren't going to fight me on it."

"On what?" I couldn't hide the confusion on

my face.

"Marriage."

"Marriage?" I asked.

"Yes."

To my surprise, the thought of matrimony no longer frightened me. I'd walked away from Damon knowing my worth and what I wanted and expecting nothing less.

I wouldn't lie to myself and discount the influence of my conversation with Mom. We'd broken down a concrete wall that seemed to have separated us from my birth. I saw her, understood her better than ever, and realized she dreamed of so much more but accepted her reality.

Her seeing a future with Damon and me meant more than I could have imagined. I fought so hard against everything about her that it felt like I'd finally done something to make her happy. It had nothing to do with her, the family, or the Morelli name.

I licked my lips and said, "It all depends on whether or not you ask me."

"First, come up here." He shifted his body and made space for me beside him.

"Why?" My heart jumped into my throat. "Are you going to propose to me in a hospital bed?"

"You won't know unless you come here."

I crawled onto the bed beside him and tucked myself against his chest. The heat of him, the feel of him, his mere presence was a comfort that filled my soul to overflowing.

"Now what?"

He brushed his mouth across my temple, letting his lips linger on my skin. I closed my eyes, taking in the scent of him.

There truly was nothing like the contentment of being in his arms. "Will you marry me, Sophia?"

"I wasn't serious." I lifted my head. "It was a joke."

"I wasn't joking." He stared at me, emotions burning in his eyes. "You're the only woman I have ever wanted to marry."

"Damon," I whispered, my throat going dry. "You're serious."

"Yes. I'm very serious." He cupped my jaw. "Do you have an answer for me?"

Swallowing, I said, "It depends. Where's the ring?

"At home, in the safe. I've had it for six weeks. Stop stalling and answer the question."

"You had a ring made for me?" My voice grew high-pitched. "But we weren't even together. Are you insane?"

He rubbed his thumb across my lower lip. "Answer my question, and I'll answer all of yours."

"Yes, I'll marry you, Damon Pierce."

CHAPTER TWENTY

Damon

I STARED DOWN at Sophia, not believing she agreed to marry me.

Tilting her face up to mine, I leaned down, brushing my lips against hers for a soft kiss before setting my head back on my pillow.

I wasn't anywhere near recovered from my concussion, so the best I could do was limit movement. However, once I was back in physical shape, this woman had a good, hard punishment coming to her, along with a brutal fucking.

"When did you order this ring for me?"

Of course, she'd caught that one specific bit of information.

"A while ago. It arrived around the time you had your encounter with the makeup artist."

"But you broke up with me or whatever that hell you put us through with that idiot thing you did in the club."

I stared up at the ceiling of the hospital room.

"I believed my whole life I came from bad blood. My grandfather and father were the worst of human beings. And being of their genetics made me no way near good enough for you.

"The kink aspect of my life wasn't an issue until Maria. Her suicide changed everything. I decided normal relationships weren't for me. Single encounters kept things safe and without consequences. But you came along."

"I do have a habit of messing up people's plans." Sophia's head settled on my chest.

"If I were a better man, I wouldn't have touched you that first night after I learned you were Lucian's sister. But you called to me on a level I never experienced. Then I fell in love with you. It was the worst thing that could possibly happen.

"I knew I would destroy your life. I not only came for the worst of humanity, but I'd engaged in things that I'd never wanted to touch you."

She opened her mouth as if to remind me of the family she came from, but I covered her lips to stop her from talking.

"Your brothers shield you from the life. Your hands have never cleaned up any of their situations. Firsthand acts are far different than living in a family where someone may or may not have engaged in nefarious activities."

She shrugged, accepting I was right.

"When the Randolph thing happened, I would have protected you through everything, sold all I had to keep the vultures away from you. That was when I knew I wanted a future and a family with you."

"You ordered the ring around that time?"

I nodded. "But I let everything with the designers and the makeup artist get in my head. It added to the scale, saying I wasn't good enough for you, and tipped it over. Or I thought."

I glanced down at her, and she met my stare. "You were most definitely wrong."

"I ruined what we had that night. I mistook your strength and trust for weakness. I took your choices from you, thinking I was doing the right thing by forcing you to walk away from a man like a man so much like my father and grandfather."

"You do know you aren't anything like them?" She asked. "I doubt they would have given up anything they wanted even if it meant it was better for the person they loved."

"They never loved anyone but themselves. On the other hand, you are the definition of self-sacrifice and love. You'll risk everything for those you love." I frowned down at her. "You know there are consequences for some of your actions from the last twenty-four hours."

"I don't recall doing anything that wasn't necessary." She tapped her chin. "I do remember saving your life."

"You could have died. Your life is more—" She covered my mouth with her palm.

"Don't you say it. If I lost you, what do you think would happen to me?" She sat up. "It's not like I'd just move on. I don't work that way."

"You are the most exasperating woman I have ever encountered."

"And you still fell in love with me. What does that say about you?"

"That I finally did something right."

✧ ✧ ✧

Sophia

"We are a go in thirty-five minutes. I need all stagehands in position. Please direct all models to their makeup stations."

I sighed, hearing the coordination manager's voice coming over my headset as I stood backstage, watching the production crew finish the final lighting adjustments for the runway show.

We were in the middle of New York Fashion

Week, and I would premiere my new collection to the world in half an hour.

I'd spent nearly every minute of the last two months since the fire at Violent Delights preparing for the event.

Now, the day was finally here, and all I wanted to do was puke.

"Breathe, you have this." Damon kissed the top of my head as my heart pounded into my ears.

"I don't know if I can do this. Walking a show is one thing, but this. What if it flops?"

"Look at me," Damon's voice grew firm, and immediately I met his emerald eyes. "You have nothing to worry about. You will shine today. I promise. Your collection represents you. Unconventional, edgy, boundary-pushing, and sexy."

I smiled. "You know how to ground me when I'm about to lose it."

"Isn't that what husbands are supposed to do?"

I glanced over at Lucian, who hadn't lost the scowl on his face since he found out Damon and I eloped over a month ago. Or maybe today's glower was because Elaine was opening the show with the piece I called "*The Virgin.*"

"He's never going to forgive you. You do know this?" Damon's amusement had me smiling.

After inviting all of the women in the family to walk the show, as expected, I received a series of nopes via their over-the-top possessive spouses. However, to my surprise, Elaine accepted and said she wanted to feel young and nothing like a mom of multiple kids.

It wasn't until after I fitted Elaine for her piece that I learned Lucian had no idea she planned to walk the runway.

"He'll get over it."

Lucian stood, focusing in on me. "Don't bet on it. My wife. The mother of my children is going to be half-naked in front of New York City because of you."

"Let me correct you." I stalked over to him and then jabbed a finger in his chest. "Elaine is going to show the world that she is a beautiful woman who has given birth, is proud of her figure, tolerates being married to you, and can rock the runway."

"You're a fucking menace, Sophia Morelli."

"Morelli-Pierce," Damon corrected from behind me, making me shake my head. "Did you forget she's married to me now? She's mine."

"Neanderthals. I'm surrounded by chest beating Neanderthals." I walked away from them and toward the prep area, where all the models were seated at makeup stations with robes covering their bodies.

I spotted Lizzy, a look of apprehension on her face.

"Hey. What's wrong?"

"What if I fall? What if I tear it? What if I—"

"Lizzy," I cut her off and took hold of her hands. "You are going to shine today."

"I shouldn't be the one going down the runway in a wedding gown. It's not like I'll ever wear something like that in real life."

I glanced at Christa, the makeup artist, signaling to give us a moment. She nodded and approached another station to talk to the model and stylist.

I lowered until I was at eye level with Lizzy.

"I said the same thing, and look where I am."

"You didn't wear a gown, remember? You wore pants with a tuxedo jacket-bustier type thing."

"True, but that's a secret, remember. As far as the family knows, you were as clueless as them."

"Yeah, yeah. To the grave."

I brushed my lips over Lizzy's forehead. "Are you ready to admit that whatever has had you all twisted up and out of sorts for the last few months has to do with a boy you met while at school?"

"Do I have to?" Her surly expression had me smiling.

"This guy really screwed you over, didn't he?"

"You don't even know the half of it," she sighed.

Even though I knew it was part of growing up, I hated to see my baby sister suffering through a broken heart. I couldn't fix this for her. It was something she'd have to figure out on her own. But I could support her in the way only a sister could.

"Fuck him. He didn't deserve you."

Her eyes widened, and she said, "You don't know the story."

"I don't need to. Anyone who hurts my sister is a jerk."

She gave me a brilliant smile. "Sophia, I don't ever want you to change. You'll take on the head of a mafia syndicate if they fucked me over, wouldn't you?"

Hell, the fuck yeah, I would.

Wait.

"Are you involved with a mob boss or something? If so, I know a few guys." I gestured with my thumb behind me to where Lucian and Damon were in a discussion or an argument about something. "They'll handle it."

Her brow furrowed. "Damon? But he's an architect."

"Among other things. He cleans up situations when necessary."

Lizzy cocked her head to the side. "And you're okay with this?"

"Why wouldn't I be? He accepts me, and I accept him."

"He's never wanted you to change?"

"Never," I answered without hesitation. "From the beginning, Damon saw me. For some reason, my attitude and smart mouth attracted him."

"So you're saying there's hope for me."

"Abso-fucking-lutely," I exclaimed. "Mr. Perfect may be sitting in that audience waiting for you to appear in that gown."

"Let's not get carried away." Lizzy laughed and then hugged me, squeezing me tight. "You do give great pep talks. I'll see you out there in a few."

I kissed her cheek and then motioned to the makeup artist to return.

Twenty-five minutes later, I stood backstage, ready to puke my guts out. The only things keeping me somewhat calm were the continuous sibling group chat updates. Leo even sent a picture of Mom and Dad in the front row of a packed to capacity showroom.

Shortly after Leo's message came one from Daphne saying, I scandalized our parents by creating a collection around the theme of BDSM and Kink. She also said it was Dad who was outraged, not Mom. She seemed excited.

If they only knew how much it meant to have both of them here. They'd come to show their support. In the grand scheme of things, Bryant and Sarah Morelli hadn't been the ideal parents, but at least they'd tried in this instance.

The first chords of the music of the evening filled the air, and the lights dimmed. The runway lit up in a silvery glow, and the spotlight centered on the opening of the stage.

Elaine waited for the show director to cue her to walk out.

She was so beautiful. The mask couldn't hide her stunning face and only added to the allure of innocence created as her blonde hair cascaded down her back in waves. Her pink and white corset accentuated her curves in all the right places. And I absolutely loved how the tutu skirt flared out around her hips, made her legs look a mile long, and helped accentuate the fuchsia stockings.

When she stepped out, I had no doubt I'd hear gasps at the exquisite way Elaine Morelli projected sin and purity. She would work the naughty virgin look like a queen.

"You're on, Elaine," I heard Aiko, my director, say just as the tempo of the trace shifted, and she was off with a flip of her hair. She took the handle of the black diamond leash attached to the choker on her neck into her hand, twirled it between her fingers, blew a kiss to Lucian, and strutted her stuff.

And as I predicted, I heard gasps and applause.

"You're a damn menace," I heard Lucian say from behind me, and I knew my security was blocking him from accessing the stage.

I lifted my head to the sky. "God, please don't let my brother ruin my show."

Five minutes later, Elaine returned, and Lucian all but threw her over his shoulder and stalked away.

"Don't leave. I need her still," I called after him, but he ignored me.

The show continued, and slowly, my nerves calmed as ten more outfits made their way down the runway without disaster.

"It's almost over. You can calm down now."

Oliana ordered as she stepped off the stage and leaned against a wall.

I had to give it to her. She wore the black and red *My Mistress* bodysuit and coat like a boss and worked the runway as if she were born into the modeling world. Only she could pull off the oversized puffer jacket and make it look sophisticated and dominatrix like. Then again, she was a fashionista and a diva.

"Lizzy is almost up. Once she goes on, and we finish. I will relax."

"I promise. You are a success."

I glared at her. "You're biased. You helped me with the project."

"And I'm one of your models." She slid a hand down her body. "I want these boots. Why didn't you tell me you were having them made for me? I would have ordered more colors."

"Focus. You're here to give me a pep talk, not ride my ass about boots."

Since she had the attention span of a gnat, she glanced to her side. "Oh look, he brought her back. Good, she isn't wrinkled. No time to steam clothes for the virgin."

The other models around us giggled, and I resisted the urge to look at Lucian and Elaine coming up behind me.

"Shut it, Dominik. I want to see my baby sister walk," Lucian took a spot near an opening to the stage.

"Go sit with the audience. We are models here," Oliana said, gesturing to everyone around her. "You can keep my Nikki company."

Lucian glared at her. "He has enough company with your entourage. I'm good here."

"So cranky. It has to be a family thing. Sophia is like this, too."

Before Lucian responded, I stepped between them and made a zip-it motion with my hands over my lips. "Shut it. I have a show in progress."

"See, cranky. Family trait."

Oh, for the love of God.

At that moment, through my earpiece, I heard Aiko instruct one of his runners to bring Lizzy out. This meant we had two minutes left.

All the blood ran out of my head, and my heartbeat pounded into my ears.

My hands shook uncontrollably.

This was it. The moment. Everything I worked for.

From the back, I heard the chatter stop, and then people stepped to the sides to let Lizzy pass.

When I saw her, tears burned the back of my eyes. She wore a hooded cap of ivory and silver covering her from head to shoulders. Small intricate patterns overlayed the material, giving it a shimmer. A rope-looking bow cinched the hood closed around her neck.

The gown she wore flowed down her body in smooth and fitted waves. From this vantage point, it resembled a high-end wedding gown worn in winter.

However, as the saying goes, looks can be deceiving.

My baby sister was breathtaking. All I could do was stare at her. I glanced to my sides and saw the same reaction on Lucian's and Elaine's faces.

"Lizzy, time to get into position," Aiko announced. "Everyone, move back. She needs space. Runners. Take your spots. You know what to do once she does her transformation thing."

I was glad I had someone like Aiko in charge. At this moment, my stomach felt as if it were eating itself.

That's when I felt his presence behind me.

"Breathe, my Sophia." Damon's palm settled on my lower back. "You've waited for this moment. Take it in."

I swallowed down my worry and watched Lizzy step out into the spotlight.

A hush grew over the crowd as if everyone was

anticipating something. Lizzy strode halfway down the runway, paused, gave everyone a sly grin, then untied the rope at her neck.

She unfurled the fabric around her head and arms, threw it high above her, and continued to walk. The material flowed in the air as if it were a cape to reveal her actual gown. Her attendants caught the cape in-flight, tugged it down, turned it into a long train, and bellowed out the full skirt of her wedding dress.

The audience erupted into cheers and claps. My heart felt as if it would explode.

Lizzy was beyond the perfect person for this dress. A silver collar encrusted with black diamonds encircled her neck. It was connected to the corseted gown by a white diamond belted chain that ran the length of her throat and between her breasts. The lacing around the waist gave Lizzy's curves an even more hourglass shape, and the crisscross pattern on the bodice mixed in with actual gems made the outfit impractical but just the right touch for a showstopper.

Lizzy grinned and then continued walking to the end of the runway. She picked up her train, allowing the cameras to capture the different angles of the dress.

Just as she turned, her attention snagged on

someone in the crowd. Instead of pausing as I expected her to do, she only blew whoever a kiss before returning to us again.

I hugged her, "Thank you, Lizzy."

"You did this, Sophia. It was you. Come on, it's time to show the world you did this."

Lizzy took my hand, pulling me toward the stage entrance.

I looked over at Damon, wanting him to be there with me.

He shook his head. "This is all you. Go shine, Sophia Donatella. I'll be here when you get back."

EPILOGUE

Damon

"IF YOU TOUCH that mask one more time, I will stop the car and tie your hands down," I said to Sophia as I turned onto the freshly paved driveway of what once used to be the Pierce estate but now was the location of mine and Sophia's new house.

It took over two years of planning, permits, and construction, but we finally finished. Today, I'd show Sophia our home, completed and ready to move in.

"I hope you know you're not my favorite person right now."

"I can live with it since the opposite is true the second any part of me is near your cunt."

"That's not a very nice word." She wrapped her arms around her growing belly. "What if they can hear you?"

I shook my head. "The only thing they can hear is your stomach noises. Besides, if they aren't bothered by me fucking you, they aren't going to care about the word cunt."

"With us as these kids' parents, one of them is destined to say shit or fuck as their first word."

"If we survived our upbringing, they will be just fine."

I pulled to a stop in front of our two-story waterfront home. This property wasn't like anything I'd ever designed. No hardlines as I would have chosen for my high rises or penthouse projects. But more on the simple elegance line, leaning toward Sophia's style.

She wanted a home, a place to feel like she belonged, to find comfort and escape the world. Until I met her, I never realized how much I needed the same thing.

Living in my penthouse for the last nearly three years wasn't so bad, but it never fit us completely.

"Why'd you stop? I swear I didn't touch the damn mask. You just want to punish me because I insisted on sleeping in the studio last night. How many times do I have to tell you, when I have a collection due, I'd rather sleep there?"

In the excitement of receiving the occupation clearance, I'd forgotten about that infraction.

"We'll address that situation later. I have

something to show you first. I'm coming around to your side. Stay in the car until I get there."

"You're so bossy."

"If you're only figuring this out now, you haven't been paying attention for the last three years." I opened the door and moved over to the passenger side. "Come with me."

I helped her up. "This is how much I trust you. I don't even question where you're taking me with a blindfold."

"You humble me."

"I drive you crazy."

"That too."

Instead of taking her into the front of the house, I led her around a patio to the back. We took a short path to a small seating area, and I turned her to face our new home.

I took a deep breath, wanting everything to be perfect for Sophia. This was a dream of hers. Every aspect of this place was a balance of our blended styles. We mixed the clean designs and geometric shapes I preferred with the elegance and pops of color and styles more in line with Sophia's taste.

There was no ice palace aesthetic anywhere.

Sophia described our style perfectly as modern elegance, with a bit of whatever the hell we liked.

This would be a place for us to live in, to grow in, laugh in, and find joy.

Tearing down the mansion that once stood here had released me from more than I could have realized. Gone was the Pierce legacy I'd carried like a weight around my neck.

Sophia and I were creating a new life and a new legacy.

We would have love here, memories, and new traditions filled with happiness.

"Take off your mask," I whispered into her ear.

"Are we having a picnic? It sounds like we're in a park." She tugged the fabric from her eyes and squinted.

As her vision adjusted, her lips trembled. "This is ours."

"Ours. And theirs." I set a hand on her stomach.

It had taken us as long to get pregnant as to build the house. When it finally happened for us, we ended up with two.

It seemed Sophia and I were never meant to have things easy, but the best things in life were worth fighting for.

✧ ✧ ✧

Thank you for reading Damon and Sienna's super steamy and emotional trilogy!

What happens to the Violent Delights club? Find out in our FREE bonus scene…
https://www.dangerouspress.com/delights

And we have more steamy Morelli books for you! You'll love Sophia's sister, Eva Morelli's story, ONE FOR THE MONEY, a fake dating billionaire romance…

Charming. Playboy. Mysterious.

Billionaire Finn Hughes hides a secret family legacy. He's as wealthy as the Rockefellers. And as powerful as the Kennedys. He runs the billion-dollar corporation. No one knows that he has a ticking time clock on his ability to lead.

Eva Morelli is the oldest daughter. The responsible one. The caring one. The one who doesn't have time for her own interests.

Especially not her interest in the charismatic, mysterious Finn Hughes.

A fake relationship is the answer to both their problems.

It will keep the swarming society mothers from throwing their daughters at him.

And it will keep Eva's mother from bothering her about marriage.

Then the fake relationship starts to feel real.

But there's no chance for them. No hope for a woman who's had her heart broken. And no future for a man whose fate was decided long ago.

The warring Morelli and Constantine families have enough bad blood to fill an ocean, and there are told by your favorite dangerous romance authors. And you can get a FREE book when you signup for our newsletter. Find out when we have new books, sales, and get exclusive bonus scenes…
www.dangerouspress.com

About Dangerous Press

The warring Morelli and Constantine families have enough bad blood to fill an ocean, and their scorching hot stories will be told by your favorite dangerous romance authors.

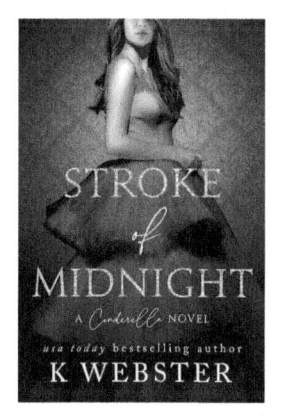

Meet Winston Constantine, the head of the Constantine family. He's used to people bowing to his will. Money can buy anything. And anyone. Including Ash Elliot, his new maid.

But love can have deadly consequences when it comes from a Constantine. At the stroke of midnight, that choice may be lost for both of them.

> "Brilliant storytelling packed with a powerful emotional punch, it's been years since I've been so invested in a book. Erotic romance at its finest!"
>
> – #1 New York Times bestselling author Rachel Van Dyken

"Stroke of Midnight is by far the hottest book I've read in a very long time! Winston Constantine is a dirty talking alpha who makes no apologies for going after what he wants."

– USA Today bestselling author
Jenika Snow

Ready for more bad boys, more drama, and more heat? The Constantines have a resident fixer. The man they call when they need someone persuaded in a violent fashion. Ronan was danger and beauty, murder and mercy.

Outside a glittering party, I saw a man in the dark. I didn't know then that he was an assassin. A hit man. A mercenary. Ronan radiated danger and beauty. Mercy and mystery.

I wanted him, but I was already promised to another man. Ronan might be the one who murdered him. But two warring families want my blood. I don't know where to turn.

In a mad world of luxury and secrets, he's the only one I can trust.

"M. O'Keefe brings her A-game in this sexy, complicated romance where you're left questioning if everything you thought was true while dying to get your hands on the next book!"

– New York Times bestselling author K. Bromberg

"Powerful, sexy, and written like a dream, RUINED is the kind of book you wish you could read forever and ever. Ronan Byrne is my new romance addiction, and I'm already pining for more blue eyes and dirty deeds in the dark."

– USA Today Bestselling Author Sierra Simone

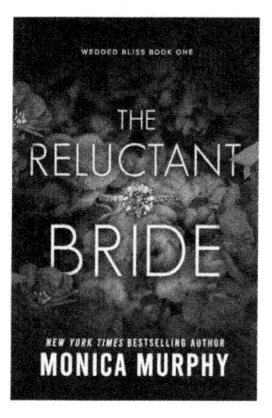

One moment I'm the forgotten daughter of one of the most wealthy families in the country, and the next I'm the blushing bride in an arranged marriage. My fate is sealed in my wedded union with a complete stranger.

"A fiery, slow burn that explodes with chemistry and achingly perfect tension. Monica Murphy has written a sizzling masterpiece."

– USA Today bestselling author Marni Mann

"Monica Murphy's The Reluctant Bride is a sinful yet sweet arranged marriage romance. I am in love with the Midnight Dynasty series!"

– USA Today Bestselling Author Natasha Knight

SIGN UP FOR THE NEWSLETTER
www.dangerouspress.com

JOIN THE FACEBOOK GROUP HERE
www.dangerouspress.com/facebook

FOLLOW US ON INSTAGRAM
www.instagram.com/dangerouspress

About the Author

USA Today Bestselling author Sienna Snow loves to serve up stories woven around confident and successful women who know what they want and how to get it, both in – and out – of the bedroom.

Her heroines are fresh, well-educated, and often find love and romance through atypical circumstances. Sienna treats her readers to enticing slices of hot romance infused with empowerment and indulgent satisfaction.

Sign up for her newsletter here: siennasnow.com/newsletter

Copyright

This is a work of fiction. Any resemblance to actual persons, living or dead, business establishments, events or locales is entirely coincidental. All rights reserved. Except for use in a review, the reproduction or use of this work in any part is forbidden without the express written permission of the author.

OWN © 2024 by Sienna Snow
Print Edition

Printed in Dunstable, United Kingdom